THE GOLDEN GNOME

A land ownership dispute and the finding of a hidden safe lead to Jennifer Beddows employing a private detective, Terry Jagger, to help investigate her grandfather's background. Together the pair uncover the secret of what lay beneath the waters of a mysterious tropical atoll and of the murders that led to its discovery.

Books by Leslie Wilkie
in the Linford Mystery Library:

THE KOKODA CONNECTION

LESLIE WILKIE

◆

THE GOLDEN GNOME

Complete and Unabridged

LINFORD
Leicester

First published in Great Britain

First Linford Edition
published 2009

British Library CIP Data

Wilkie, Leslie.
   The golden gnome
   1. Private investigators- -Fiction.
   2. Land tenure- -Tropics- -Fiction.
   3. Family secrets- -Fiction. 4. Suspense fiction.
   5. Large type books.
   I. Title
   823.9'2–dc22

   ISBN 978–1–84782–715–9

Published by
F. A. Thorpe (Publishing)
Anstey, Leicestershire

Set by Words & Graphics Ltd.
Anstey, Leicestershire
Printed and bound in Great Britain by
T. J. International Ltd., Padstow, Cornwall

This book is printed on acid-free paper

To my wife Joan and my daughters
Colette, Alison and Deborah
With love

Acknowledgements

My thanks to Lesley for her editorial efforts and to all those members of the Driffield Writers Group past and present who have read, endured and offered constructive criticism of my work.

1

I once asked Charlie Foster who Bemrose, Potts and Smythe were and apart from Potts he hadn't a clue. Potts was the old man Charlie acquired the business from but by the time he took over Bemrose and Smythe had long gone to their maker. Charlie still operates under the full title but he's the only solicitor left in the office. It was his secretary, Janice, who rang me that morning last year. She said he needed me for a small local job. As it turned out she couldn't have been more wrong.

Who am I? — Terry Jagger, an ex naval officer with what one might call some 'independent means'. My Uncle George, a rogue with a talent for making money, left me part of his substantial estate when he died. He left it in the form of an annual allowance to prevent me blowing his hard-earned cash in one massive binge. It's not enough for me to live on but it does allow me some leeway, I can pick and choose my work to suit my mood. I'm thirty-four years old, six feet tall with rather battered features. Women seem to find me attractive but I've no idea why. I'm single and I'm told that I've left one or two broken hearts behind on my travels. If I have it's purely unintentional.

I've done several jobs for Charlie, mainly ones that involve overseas travel and investigation. His client base is largely expatriate although a few of the local clients he inherited from Potts are still on his books. It was one of those local clients that required my help that morning.

'It's something to do with missing title deeds,' said Charlie. 'I'd go myself but I've got a case at Hull Crown Court this morning so can you cover for me?'

I reluctantly agreed and took down the name and address. Charlie and I live in the East Yorkshire market town of Beverley and the address he gave me was in a village some ten miles away, a village called Little Driffield.

It took me a while to find the property because although the address indicated that the house was in the village it was actually about half a mile outside. When I arrived I found a confrontation taking place between a young woman and three men. A car blocked the driveway. I parked at the side of the road and walked across to the group. The name I had been given was Miss Jennifer Beddows and somehow I had been expecting to find an old spinster but the woman standing by the car couldn't have been more than mid twenties. Ignoring the men I addressed myself to her.

'Miss Beddows?'

'Yes, who are you?' She asked rather curtly.

'My name is Jagger, I represent Bemrose, Potts and Smythe. I understand you need some assistance.'

'Thank goodness you've come.' She softened her tone and gave a tentative smile.

Taking her arm I led her round the car and out of the hearing of the three men.

'Tell me quickly what the problem is.'

'Those men are from Blassets builders. They're developing a site at the rear of my house and claim that part of my garden is their land. They're trying to fence off part of my land today. The trouble is I can't find the title deeds to this property to disprove their claim.'

'Okay, let's get rid of these guys first then we'll worry about title deeds.'

I walked back to the group by the car.

'Who are you?' I asked, eyeing each of them in turn.

'I'm Morris, site foreman,' said one.

'And these two gentlemen?' I asked, nodding towards his compatriots.

'Labourers, they've to sort out the new fence.'

'Right Mr Morris and you two gentlemen, I want it clearly understood that if you put one foot onto this property you will be charged with trespass. Also, if so much as one blade of grass is touched you will be charged with causing malicious damage.' I put my hand into my inside pocket and took out a folded sheaf of papers. 'I have a court order forbidding any intrusion onto this land until the subject of title has been settled. Do you understand?'

'We're only trying to do our job,' muttered Morris.

'So am I Mr Morris, so am I.'

I watched as the three men walked off along the road. Behind me Jennifer Beddows asked, 'How could you get a court order?'

'Court order?'

'Yes, that thing in your hand.'

'Ah, you must have misunderstood me. This is a list of Yorkshire County Cricket fixtures,' I said passing the papers to her.

'But won't they find out that you haven't got a court order?' She protested.

'Possibly, but I doubt if they'll do so today so we'd better get to work and find your title deeds. If you'll move your car I'll bring mine onto the drive.'

A few minutes later, with both cars parked in front of the house, Jennifer Beddows led me inside. The house was built in a mock Tudor style and proved to be fairly substantial. I was given a quick tour of the ground floor and in addition to a large kitchen I counted four other rooms, all of them spacious when compared to their modern day equivalent. A wide curved staircase led to the upper floors. The guided tour finished in a study cum library.

'This was my Grandfather's room,' said Jennifer.

'Is this where the house deeds would normally be kept?' I asked.

'I don't know. I've never seen them.'

'Is there anyone else, your parents perhaps?'

'No, I live alone. Both my parents are dead. They were killed in a road accident shortly after Grandfather died.'

'When was this?'

'About six years ago — November 1999. When Grandfather died Daddy dealt with your Mr Potts and I dealt with him when Daddy was killed.'

'Mr Potts is no longer with the firm I'm afraid and, as I understand it, there are no deeds lodged in our office. Have you tried the bank, they may have them in safe keeping?'

'No, I tried them first.'

'Is there a safe in the house?'

'No.'

'Have you searched the house thoroughly?'

'I've looked in all the drawers and cupboards.'

'The desk?' I asked.

'There were some of Daddy's papers there and a copy of Grandfather's will but apart from bills there was nothing else.'

'Did your Grandfather travel abroad?'

'Yes, that's where he made his money.'

'Where was his passport kept?'

'I've never seen it. I know Daddy was puzzled about that and by the lack of insurance papers.'

'Well, I assume there's a hiding place somewhere which you haven't found. Do you want me to search the house?'

'Yes please.'

'May I start in this room?'

She nodded assent.

I started with the desk, taking the drawers out one by one searching for any sign of a hiding place. I did find a concealed drawer but all it held was a pewter hip flask half full of whiskey. At the end of four hours I was still working in that room. I was covered in dust with cobwebs stuck in my hair and I hadn't found a thing. Several hundred books lay in piles here and there and pictures were propped against various pieces of furniture. I had crawled round the room looking for trapdoors concealed under carpets, tapped my way round the plaster and panelling of the walls, all to no avail.

The breakthrough, when it came, was a fluke; I was replacing books onto their respective shelves when I caught my hand on what appeared to be a raised knot in the woodwork. On closer examination it turned out to be a push button cleverly painted to resemble a knot, when I pressed it, a section of shelving slid back to reveal a hidden safe. There was a combination lock and it was firmly secured.

Jennifer had left me to the search some time earlier and was astounded to see the safe when I called her.

'Can you open it?' she asked.

'I need the combination. Have you any suggestions?'

'No I haven't.'

'How about trying your Grandfather's birthday?'

I spent an hour turning the dial backwards and forwards trying various permutations of family birthdays and any other collections of numbers that I and Jennifer felt might be relevant, without success. We were sitting drinking coffee prior to restoring the room to its normal tidy state when I spotted a series of numbers we hadn't tried. A painting of a cruising yacht in full sail had a small brass plate attached to the frame. The plate bore the name and a six-figure registration number of the vessel.

'Whose yacht is it?' I asked.

'It's Grandfather's.'

'Let's try that number then.'

It worked. I don't know what I was expecting to see as I opened the safe door but I certainly wasn't expecting a minature garden gnome. It was about four inches tall, gold in colour and it appeared to be standing guard over several documents, some of which were tied with red ribbon. I stepped back and allowed Jennifer to investigate the contents. I think she was also slightly taken aback by the gnome at first but once she had regained her composure she sifted quickly through the documents. The title deeds and land registry certificates for the house were there.

Spreading the deeds out on the desk Jennifer selected the map showing the boundaries of the property. She pointed to the field behind her home.

'That's the field that Blassets are working on. Their map shows a completely square field but as you can see from this, my map shows it differently. The garden at the back here protrudes into the bottom corner of that field.'

'The land registry stamp says 1985, has there been any change since then?'

'No, that's when my Grandfather bought this place and it's always been the same.'

'If you've no objection I'd like to walk down the garden and see just what Blassets are up to.'

'I'll come with you,' she said. 'I'll just put this lot away first.' She gathered together all the various documents and replaced them in the safe. I watched her touch the gnome, turn it into the light and give it a curious look.

'Have you seen it before,' I asked.

'Only in books,' she replied. 'I think it's one of the seven dwarfs.'

She locked the safe, pressed the hidden button and watched as the section of shelving slid back into place.

'My Grandfather was a very secretive person,' she said in an undertone, as if talking to herself. She looked up at me, a thoughtful expression on her face then she smiled and said, 'Let's go.'

The upper part of the rear garden was a virtual forest of trees and shrubs with a brick path winding through them so it wasn't until we were halfway down it that I saw the boat. It stood on wooden trestles in the bottom right hand corner. I estimated it to be about forty feet long. The hull towered over us. To one side was a set of smaller trestles holding what I assumed were the masts and spars.

'How on earth did he get that down here?' I exclaimed.

'I never saw it but I'm told it was brought across that field on a low-loader

11

and lifted by crane onto those trestles. They laid portable metal tracks so that the machines didn't sink.'

'Why did he want it here?'

'Two reasons, one because he thought the mooring charges were exorbitant and secondly because he wanted to work on it.'

'I'd like to see her back in the water.' I said.

'Do you sail?'

I nodded. 'I used to be a sailor. It looks as though she'll need some TLC now before she goes back to sea.'

I stood and studied the stranded vessel. Tarpaulins were tied over her upperworks and these were streaked white with years of accumulated bird droppings. Where the securing ropes had slackened the tarpaulin had sagged allowing pools of stagnant water to accumulate. Rust streaks ran down the exposed hull and in places patches of paint had flaked away. She looked in a sorry state.

'It doesn't look as if he did much work on her.'

'He did at first,' said Jennifer. 'That's

his workshop over there.'

She pointed to the opposite side of the garden where a substantial brick structure was almost hidden in overhanging trees.

'I used to come down here when I was a teenager. There's a metalwork room with a forge and another room with a lathe and drills. He did a lot of work inside the boat.'

The garden was fully enclosed by twelve to fifteen feet high Leylandii, the quick growing evergreen trees that have recently become the subject of new legislation. They are grown to give privacy but what is privacy to some is a damn nuisance to others. In this case they had been planted so close together that they formed a solid green wall. I couldn't see into the adjoining field.

Jennifer led the way round the stern of the yacht to where two of the trees had been planted slightly out of line with the rest leaving a narrow gap for us to squeeze through. Once in the field I could see immediately that the area of garden holding the yacht and the workshop protruded into it. Fortunately there were no workmen around to confront us so we explored their site without interruption. There wasn't much to see; just a six feet deep ditch cut diagonally across the field guarded by a silent JCB and a bulldozer. The only other indication of work in progress was a pile of new fence posts lying by the gate. Pinned to the gatepost was a planning notice and I took down the details so that I could find out just what was to happen to the site.

Back at the house I telephoned Charlie Foster and brought him up to date with the day's events including my 'court order' statement. Charlie's court case had resulted in his client being placed on remand for several weeks leaving Charlie free the following day. That left him the opportunity to take over from me. After making sure that Jennifer Beddows could open the safe again, and showing her how to alter the combination if she so desired, I drove home.

2

Ten days after my visit to the home of Jennifer Beddows, Charlie rang me again. This time he wanted to see me in the office. I arranged to meet him early the following morning but he failed to mention that it was Jennifer who had asked for the meeting. She arrived shortly after me and we were both there before Charlie. He arrived a few minutes later complaining bitterly about the density of the rush hour traffic. I think he'd been snarled up in the school run. He waved us through into his office and continued to prattle on about the traffic until Janice arrived with coffee for the three of us. He then got straight down to business.

'Finding that safe has given us more problems than it has solved,' he said, looking across the desk at me.

'But I thought we'd found the deeds.' I protested.

He nodded. 'That's true and they're

not the problem anymore. Blassets have admitted their mistake. All they are doing is running a gas pipeline across that field for a company called Eronogis. Eronogis are the French subsidiary of a German energy company and they have outline planning permission to build a gas pumping station on that land sometime in the future.'

'Then what is the problem?'

'My Grandfather's will,' said Jennifer. 'There's a lot that doesn't make sense.' She turned to Charlie. 'You'd better explain.'

'You have to understand,' said Charlie, 'that Albert Beddows appears to have been a very secretive man. He can't have told his son, Jennifer's father, about the safe. I'm sure he intended to but died before doing so.'

'How did he die?' I asked.

'Brain haemorrhage. He collapsed in the street and was dead before they got him to hospital.'

Charlie went on to explain that Albert's will had left everything he owned to his son David but if David predeceased

Albert then Jennifer was the sole beneficiary. As it happened David died only weeks after his father and Jennifer inherited from both of them.

'I still can't see the problem.' I said when Charlie paused for breath.

'Albert left all his property 'at home and overseas' to David but David didn't know there was any overseas property. He'd queried this with my predecessor but I think old man Potts had filed it under 'too hard'. You must remember that Potts and his secretary were one step from senility when I took over. I've been finding unfinished business like this ever since.'

'What have you found in the safe?'

'Details of a Swiss bank account, another account in the Fijian branch of an Australian bank and what appears to be the deeds of property in the Kingston Islands.'

'Where?'

'The Kingston Islands.'

'Never heard of them.'

'I can't find any reference to them either,' said Jennifer.

17

'There's one other thing.' Charlie got to his feet and walked across to a safe in the corner of the office. Opening it he took out an object wrapped in cloth. Setting it down on the desk he removed the wrapping to reveal the golden coloured figure that I'd seen in Jennifer's safe.

'I believe you called it a garden gnome. Jennifer thought it was one of the seven dwarfs. You are both wrong, it's made of pure gold, has Russian assay marks and was last reported to be in Poland before the second world-war. It's part of a chess set.'

'A chess set!' exclaimed Jennifer.

'It was originally owned by a Count Boronofski, a minor member of the Russian court. It disappeared at the time of the revolution then resurfaced in Poland some years later. When the Germans invaded Poland in the war it went missing again. This is the first time any part of it has reappeared since.'

I reached across the desk and picked up the piece. The workmanship was superb, it was the figure of an old man

18

and the features of the lined face were almost lifelike.

'What part of the chess set is it?'

'I'm told it's one of the pawns,' replied Charlie.

'How much is it worth?' Jennifer asked.

'On its own, about four thousand pounds but the full set would be worth millions.'

'Is there anything in the safe that indicates where he got it from?' I said, replacing the figure back in front of Charlie.

'No, nothing.'

'Surely they can't all be that colour,' Jennifer interjected.

Charlie nodded. 'You're right, the gold ones are the black pieces and the white are made of silver.'

'Where did you get your information from Charlie?' I asked.

'A contact of mine in the antiques business.'

'A trustworthy one?'

'I believe so.'

I sat back and looked across at Jennifer. 'What happens now?' I asked.

'I'm flying to Switzerland tomorrow to investigate this bank account of Grandfather's. The bankers refuse to discuss it by phone and they need to see the will and death certificates before they'll consider my claim.'

'What do you want me to do?'

'I'd like you to look over the yacht. It's no use to me so I'm thinking of selling it. Would it be worth selling it as it is or should I have it moved to a marina and cleaned up first?'

'Well I'm not a yacht valuer but I'll certainly look it over and give you my opinion.'

'When could you start?'

'Today if you like, I'll have to change into some working clothes, how about after lunch?'

She glanced at her watch before replying. 'I could provide a working lunch,' she said. 'Beer and sandwiches?'

'Yes that'll do fine. I'll pick up some working gear and meet you at the house in about an hour.'

She smiled and nodded her agreement. Turning to Charlie, I spotted the hint of a knowing smile on his face as I asked if he had any more to add.

'No,' he said. 'Just keep me informed of any developments.'

I didn't bother changing at home so I arrived at Jennifer's house within the hour. My working gear consisted of a pair of jeans, a denim shirt and a pair of rope-soled deck shoes. As I collected them from the back seat of my car Jennifer called me from an upstairs window.

'The door's open.'

'Where can I change?'

'Come on up, I'll show you.'

She met me at the top of the stairs and directed me towards a bathroom. When I emerged a few minutes later Jennifer was waiting for me by the staircase, she was also dressed in old clothing but hers were liberally daubed in paint. I forget now what I said but it was something to do with the paint.

'It's my work,' she said. 'I'm a painter.'

'Artistic painter?'

'I illustrate children's books.'

'Do you work from home?'

21

'Yes, I turned one of the bedrooms into a studio.'

She led the way out into the garden collecting a bunch of keys from a hook in the kitchen en route.

'These are the keys to the workshop and the boat. There's a ladder in the workshop which you'll need to get up onto the deck.'

'Are you coming aboard with me?'

'No, I've got a painting to finish and some packing to do. I'll show you where things are then get back to work. If you come back up to the house about one o'clock I'll have lunch ready.'

The ladder was a lightweight aluminium one and I soon had it safely rigged. However, the tarpaulins were a tougher proposition. The securing ropes had set hard round the cleats, cemented in place by bird droppings. Once I had struggled to clear them I drained the accumulated rainwater over the side and folded the tarpaulins back away from the cabin. Stepping into the cockpit I found that the companionway was locked. Jennifer had warned me that it probably would be and I quickly found the required key. As soon as I opened the hatchway a waft of stale air brought with it a smell of diesel and paint. I allowed it to clear for a few minutes before moving below and opening skylights and the fore hatch to allow fresh air to circulate.

I had brought a small notebook with me and I sat in sunshine on the foredeck making notes of what I had already discovered about the boat. She was called *Island Beauty* and her port of registry was Auckland, New Zealand. She had a wooden hull and the long keel typical of some ocean cruisers. She was built for endurance rather than speed and had a cutter rig with the cockpit positioned aft. The information about the sail arrangement came from what I remembered of the painting in the study.

Moving below decks I noted five berths, two in the forepeak, two in the main cabin and a quarter berth. No attempt had been made to stow away loose equipment and that puzzled me. Binoculars, compass, radios, a sextant and cooking utensils still stood on shelves held in place by fiddles. There were even small objects like pencils and dividers lying on the chart table. In the galley there were tinned and dried foods in cupboards and a particularly evil looking lump of mould in the fridge, the sails weren't properly stowed, merely bundled in heaps on top of the forepeak berths. It was as if the old man had lost all interest in the boat as soon as it was lifted out of the water. However, I distinctly remembered Jennifer telling me that he had done a lot of work on her. I couldn't see where.

My watch confirmed what my stomach had been telling me for a while, that it was time to seek out some lunch. I was about to descend the ladder when Jennifer appeared in the garden below.

'I thought you'd forgotten lunch,' she called.

'Just coming.'

As we walked back to the house together I asked her what kind of work her Grandfather had done on the boat.

'Some kind of metal work, I never went onboard while he was working but I do remember him doing some welding. The welding equipment is still in the work-shop.'

Over lunch we discussed her trip to Zurich the following day. She was leaving the house early and driving to Humber-side Airport in order to catch the first flight to Amsterdam. After changing aircraft in Schipol she would be due to arrive in Zurich shortly after lunch. Her appointment at the bank was for nine o'clock the following morning and if all went well she was hoping to catch the last flight from Amsterdam that night.

It may be odd but during that scratch meal I suddenly began to see Jennifer as very attractive. Until then she'd been a client but sitting across the table from her that lunchtime I began to see her in a different light. I don't know what it was that changed my perception of her but I began to like what I was seeing. Her hair was jet black and swung free just above her shoulders. She wore no makeup and her creamy coloured skin contrasted with her black eyelashes and green eyes. There was a smudge of blue paint above her right eye where she had obviously brushed her hair back while she was painting and for one moment I was tempted to lean across and brush it away. I resisted.

I was still thinking about her as I climbed back aboard the yacht. However, it was what she had said before lunch about the welding that was intriguing me. In my brief tour of the accommodation I'd seen no sign of any work of that nature but then I hadn't yet investigated the engine compartment, fuel tanks, bilge pump or the heads. My intention was to leave that until the following day. What I had in mind for the rest of the afternoon was to thoroughly search the accommodation and navigation area for any reference to the Kingston Islands. I'd seen a chart drawer earlier but hadn't opened it and there were also a number of pilot books in a rack above the chart table. The one other thing I was hoping to find was a logbook.

It took me most of the afternoon to trace the last voyage of the *Island Beauty* and I had to do it without the logbook.

Although I searched the accommodation thoroughly I never found it. However, the thirty-two charts told a story of a voyage halfway round the world. The pencilled courses and positions marked on the top three charts led back from Hull to the first landfall in the U.K. — St Peter Port in Guernsey. As an ex-naval officer I found the practice of leaving the courses and positions marked on the charts unusual. I had always been taught to erase all such marks at the end of the voyage leaving things clean for the next time they were required. In this case some charts had been cleaned but not all.

There was no lighting available in the accommodation so I carried the charts out onto the deck in order to trace the voyage. On those charts where the courses had been erased the faint indentations of the pencil still remained allowing me to follow the vessel's track. It led back across the Atlantic via the Azores and the Caribbean to the Panama Canal. On the Pacific side of the Canal I followed the faint position marks to the Galapogos Islands and west across the ocean. I lost the track for a time before picking it up again near Fiji. From there the course went north for some distance before suddenly reversing and heading south to New Zealand. I failed to find any reference to the Kingston Islands on any of the charts.

It was mid afternoon before I put the charts aside and began the structural assessment of the yacht. The lack of internal lights made things difficult especially in the engine compartment. The engine itself was quite a powerful looking diesel and I judged it to be bigger than would be required for harbour manoeuvring, big enough to push the boat along at a fair speed if required. The fuel tank was larger than I would have expected and to my astonishment was still half full of diesel. It was the same with the fresh water tanks — water still remained in them. Had I been laying up such a vessel I would have made sure that not only were the tanks drained but they were also cleaned before any attempt was made to lift it out of the water.

The sun disappeared behind a thin veil

of cloud about four o'clock making it even more difficult to see what I was doing inside the yacht. I gave up then, closed the skylights and fore hatch and locked the companionway entrance. Leaving the tarpaulins rolled back I returned the ladder to the workshop before going in search of Jennifer. She was in the kitchen.

'Finished?' she asked.

'No, there are no lights onboard so it's difficult to see inside. I'd like to come back tomorrow with a torch and have another go.'

'You'd better hang on to those keys then because I'm leaving early tomorrow.'

'Thank you. Tell me, did your Grandfather sail that yacht alone?'

'No, he had a New Zealand couple with him. There's a book in the safe with their names in it. Would you like to see it?'

'Please.'

'I'll leave it out here on the table. You've got a spare set of house keys on that bunch.'

On my way home I called in at the

library in the hope of finding some reference to the Kingston Islands. Even they couldn't help me. There were plenty of Kingstons including Kingston upon Hull where Albert Beddows was born but no Kingston Islands.

3

The following morning I arrived at the empty house just after ten. Using the spare set of keys that Jennifer had given me I let myself in and walked through to the kitchen. On the table lay the book and a short note telling me to help myself to tea or coffee. The book was what I was hoping to see, the logbook of *Island Beauty*. It was a relatively new logbook covering just the last voyage from Auckland. I made myself a cup of instant coffee — there was a percolator but I was eager to read the details of that last voyage so I stuck to the Fair Trade instant for convenience.

Jennifer's Grandfather, Albert Beddows, set sail from Auckland on his own and headed almost due north. His track took him between the island groups of Fiji and Vanuatu and on past the Solomon islands to a point northwest of Tuvalu. He sailed north for twelve days and the logbook duly recorded the boat's position, course and speed and little else apart from brief details of weather conditions. On the thirteenth day however came the entry I'd been hoping to find. It read, '0915 local time anchored K.I.'. That had to be the Kingston Islands.

There was an atlas in the study but when I checked the position given in the logbook with the map of the Pacific Islands there was no sign of those islands. Where the Kingston Islands were supposed to be was just open water. It was obvious that I needed a large-scale chart of the area so I made my way down the garden and climbed aboard the yacht. I found the chart I needed and plotted the logbook position carefully. The chart showed the symbols for dangerous reefs in exactly that position.

Back out on deck I sat in the warm morning sunshine and continued to read through the logbook. I couldn't understand why Albert had sailed single-handed for such a long distance. He'd spent almost a fortnight at sea en-route to what he called the Kingston Islands, then seven days at anchor before reversing his course to Fiji. There, in the port of Suva, the New Zealand couple had boarded the yacht. Why hadn't they gone aboard in Auckland? Had Albert something to hide in those mysterious islands of his, I wondered? Eventually I decided that there was no point in trying to guess what Albert's reasons were and I put aside the logbook and got on with the job I was supposed to be doing, assessing the condition of the yacht.

It was mid afternoon when I spotted the newish looking welding in the engine compartment. There were four tubular stanchions that were probably put in place to provide extra support for the engine. I could see that the original engine had been removed at some time in the past and this larger engine installed but what I couldn't understand was why those stanchions had the appearance of being recently removed and replaced. Then I remembered what Jennifer had said about the work Albert had done. I must confess I was intrigued by what I'd

33

found so I decided to investigate the workshop to see if there was any clue there.

There were two main rooms in the workshop plus a small storage locker. One room was virtually a blacksmith's shop with a furnace, anvil and heavy metal-working tools. The other was equipped with a small lathe, a power saw and an electric drill mounted on a bench. In this room were all the smaller, finer tools and the welding gear. One thing I hadn't expected to find was another safe. This one was an old fashioned key locking type and it was securely bolted to the concrete floor. It was locked.

In the storage locker I discovered a black plastic rubbish bag holding what looked to be asbestos packing material. I was about to put it aside when I suddenly realised that the packing was tubular in shape and about the same diameter as that newly welded pipework in the engine compartment on the yacht. I'd seen a pair of working gloves on the bench so I put those on before investigating that packing. I lifted it out piece by piece and spread it on the bench. Then, as if putting together a jigsaw, I tried matching each broken piece. Eventually I finished up with four tubular sections that appeared to fit the rewelded stanchions perfectly. After that it didn't take me long to speculate on the possibility that Albert had been bringing something into the country by illegal means. He'd hidden something in each of the four stanchions after wrapping it securely in the packing material.

The more I thought about it the more I began to realise what had happened on that final voyage. Albert obviously wanted to bring something into this country by illegal means and that something was kept on the Kingston Islands. That would explain why he'd sailed on his own from Auckland to the islands. In the week that he'd spent there he must have hidden his mysterious hoard in those stanchions before reversing his track to Fiji and picking up the New Zealanders. He obviously didn't want those two to know what he'd hidden aboard the yacht. Once back in England he'd had the yacht brought to its present site in the garden so that he could retrieve whatever he had hidden in privacy.

Leaving the packing material on the bench I returned to the yacht. I'd remembered seeing a number of pilot books in the cabin and I was hoping that one of them would hold more information on the islands. Taking the relevant book out on deck I sat in the warm sunshine while I searched. There was no mention of the Kingston Islands but listed for the position shown on the chart was a brief note. It read 'Atoll 437 U.S. Navy'. An atoll meant islands, not just dangerous reefs. What on earth, I wondered, was Albert doing on islands that were apparently owned by the United States Navy Department?

Because of my own naval service I still maintained contact with a small number of friends who were in the Royal Navy. One of them, Commander Stuart Gibson, was currently assigned to a shore-based position in the hydrographic service. I decided to contact him to see if he could enlighten me about Atoll 437. He wasn't in his office when I rang so I left my mobile number with a request that he contacted me. He rang back a few minutes later.

'Why is it whenever I hear the name Terry Jagger I suspect trouble?'

'What, not even a good afternoon how are you?' I replied.

He chuckled. 'Okay you old bugger, what is it you want this time?'

'I'd like to know how Christine and the boys are.'

'Christine is fine, enjoying life in England once again, Bill is in his first year at university and David is as dizzy as ever. Now, why did you really ring me?'

'For a little bit of info.'

I explained about Albert Beddow's will and about the Kingston Islands. I told him the charted position and explained how I'd come to the conclusion that Albert's islands and the U.S. Navy's Atoll 437 appeared to be the same place. I did not mention that I suspected Albert of smuggling.

'If this place is owned by the U.S. Navy

any information about it is likely to be classified.'

'Yes I know, but I would appreciate anything you can find out about the place for me.'

'Okay, I'll give it a go. I'll ring you if I find anything.'

'Thanks Stuart, give my love to Christine.'

'Not on your life, I'll give her your regards and my love,' he said with a chuckle. He was still laughing when the line went dead.

I remained on deck for a further fifteen minutes writing up my notes on the condition of the yacht. As far as I could tell she was in remarkably good condition. She certainly needed some external spit and polish and the engine would need a service but otherwise she seemed to be okay. In fact the more I wrote about her the more I longed to see her back in the water where she belonged.

Later, after locking the boat and returning the ladder to the shed, I went back to the house. Leaving the logbook where I had found it on the kitchen table

I wrote a quick note asking Jennifer to ring me when she returned. Throughout the drive home I couldn't get my suspicions about Albert's activities out of my mind, should I tell Jennifer about them or not? In the end I decided that she had to know.

4

Stuart rang me early the next day. He'd probably been at his desk for nearly an hour but I was still finishing my breakfast. Once again there were no preliminary greetings he went straight into the business of the day.

'I've got that info you wanted,' he said. 'Technically the atoll is still U.S. Navy property but it hasn't been used for nearly sixty years. It was abandoned shortly after the second-world-war.'

'What did they use it for?'

'I'm told it was an emergency landing strip.'

'But the chart I've got seems to suggest that there's little more than reefs there now.'

'There were two islands just a few feet above the high water mark. One was used as the landing strip and the men lived on the other. Since then of course nature has taken over and the sea has virtually reclaimed them.'

'Is that the result of global warming?'

'More or less, the islands are still there but they are only about half their original size.'

'Is there any mention of them being called 'The Kingston Islands'?'

'None whatsoever.'

'Well, thanks Stuart. May I ask where you got this information from?'

'A friend of mine in the U.S. Naval Attaché's office in London.'

'Thanks again. Did you pass on my love to Christine?'

'No, just your regards.'

It's odd isn't it how once you acquire a reputation as a Casanova, however unjustified it may be, it takes forever to live it down. In my case it occurred just a couple of years before I left the navy. A certain married lady who was already in the process of divorcing her husband because of his philandering, decided that what was good for the gander was also good for the goose. I just happened to be her target. I must admit I didn't discourage her and, judging by Stuart's comments, the reputation I'd acquired as a result was still with me. Incidentally, the lady in question went on to marry a second husband only a few months later, and as far as I know, she's still married. I obviously didn't do her reputation any harm.

Turning my mind back to the boat I decided to check what facilities were available locally for lifting her back into the water. I'd seen a large boat hoist in Bridlington harbour that could probably do the job but I also knew that there must be one available at Hull marina. I decided to find out more about the marina's facilities first since that was a specialist yachting centre whereas I suspected Bridlington was a commercial fishing port first and foremost. A telephone call to the marina office in Hull put me in contact with a lady called Julie who assured me that the marina had a 50 ton boat hoist available. When I explained why I needed the information she agreed to send me details of the marina and boatyard facilities and services. I did consider getting a quote for moving the boat to the marina from a specialist contractor but I opted to leave that until Jennifer returned.

After lunch I decided to drive out to Jennifer's home once again. There was nothing more that I could really do until she returned from Switzerland but something drew me back there. I didn't enter the house. I merely walked round it and down the garden to the boat. Taking the ladder from the workshop I climbed aboard, opened the skylights and fore-hatch and then began to put things shipshape. I dragged the tangle of sails from the forepeak and dropped them over the side into the garden. It took me the best part of an hour to tidy them up and stow them back on board. Then I turned my attention to the fresh water tank allowing the water to drain overboard before flushing the tank clean with a hosepipe I'd found in the workshop. There was nothing I could do about the diesel tank that would have to stay as it was until the contents could be drained off into a tanker. It was while I was checking through the tinned and dried foodstuff that I heard a shout from below.

I moved out on deck and peered over the rail. Jennifer had returned earlier than anticipated.

'I wasn't expecting to find you here but I'm glad you are. I've asked Mr Foster to come out here and I'd like you to join us,' she called.

'Charlie's coming here, when?'

'In about fifteen minutes.'

'Okay, I'll lock up and be with you shortly.'

In the time it took me to tidy up and stow away the ladder Jennifer had made coffee and Charlie had arrived. They were both seated at the kitchen table when I walked in. I was still in my working gear and I remember apologising for my scruffy state as I washed my hands at the kitchen sink. I was taking my place at the table when Charlie asked Jennifer about her trip.

'The actual journey was fine,' she replied. 'It was what I found at the bank that stunned me.'

'I presume they accepted your claim,' said Charlie.

'Once they'd seen the death certificates

and the will there was no problem. I've given the bank your office details because there is still some paperwork to be finalised.'

'Is that why you called me here?' Charlie asked.

'Partly, but I cannot understand what I found, so I'd like you to do some investigation for me.'

'Investigation, into what?'

'My Grandfather's background.'

Charlie looked across at me. 'This sounds like your kind of thing,' he said.

Jennifer opened her handbag, removed a small twist of tissue paper and passed it across to me. 'Open it,' she said, 'then tell me what you think.'

Inside, on a small pad of cottonwool lay three stones, gem stones. I picked up what I took to be a superbly cut diamond and held it up to the light.

'Diamond?' I asked.

Jennifer nodded, then pointing to the remaining stones she said, 'Emerald and ruby.'

I looked across at her but I didn't have to ask the question.

45

'They were in a safe deposit box at the bank along with nearly one hundred others. I just don't understand where he got them. In addition,' she continued, 'there's almost two hundred thousand pounds in Swiss francs. I thought his background was in engineering. Where does an engineer come by that kind of money?'

'The money could have been his pension fund,' said Charlie thoughtfully. 'As for the stones I couldn't hazard a guess.'

'The answer probably lies in the Kingston Isles,' I muttered, more to myself than the others. 'Don't forget there's also the chess piece.'

I paused and looked up. 'I think that's where he got the stones and possibly the chess piece. What else did he smuggle in?'

'Smuggle, what on earth are you talking about?' Charlie exclaimed.

I glanced across at him and then transferred my gaze to Jennifer. 'I'm sorry it's my theory on why your Grandfather was so interested in the Kingston Islands.'

'Have you found the islands then?' She asked.

'I think so.'

I began to explain how I'd tracked the last voyage of the *Island Beauty* using the charts onboard the yacht. When I reached the part about the chart showing dangerous reefs instead of islands Jennifer interrupted me.

'I'm finding it hard to visualise all these places you've mentioned. I'd find it much easier if I could see the charts.'

'They're still onboard the yacht,' I said. 'Do you want me bring them down here.'

'What evidence have you got to support this smuggling theory?'

'That's on the yacht as well but I can't bring that down here.'

Jennifer turned to address Charlie. 'Have you got time to spare?'

He nodded then glanced at his watch. 'Yes I'm okay for about half an hour,' he replied.

'Right then let's go and see what Terry has found.'

I picked up the logbook from the table. 'We'll need this,' I said.

Ten minutes later the three of us were seated round the table in the saloon of

Island Beauty. Using both the logbook entries and the appropriate charts I showed them the yacht's track back from the U.K. to where the chart showed the dangerous reefs. Then I explained about the two small islands and how the U.S. Navy had utilised them during the second-world-war. At the point Jennifer interrupted me.

'There's a document in the safe with United States Navy markings. I haven't had chance to study it yet: everything's happened so quickly since you found the safe.'

'That reminds me,' I said. 'I've found another one.'

'Another safe?'

'Yes, in the workshop, I'll show you later.'

After that I explained how her grandfather had sailed from Auckland on his own and had voyaged north for almost two weeks to reach the islands. Then, after spending a week there, he'd reversed his track to Fiji where the two New Zealanders joined him.

'My theory is that he sailed alone in

order to collect something from what he calls the Kingston Islands without anyone else knowing about it. I think that 'something' may well be those gemstones and the chess piece,' I said.

'Proof?' Charlie queried.

'Jennifer told me that her grandfather had brought the yacht here to work on it and that work had involved some welding. The only evidence of new welding I can find is in the engine compartment. Come, I'll show you.'

There was barely room for two of us to squeeze into the engine space together so I had to go through my routine twice. Charlie wasn't particularly impressed at first but when I tapped the tubular stanchions with a spanner to demonstrate that they were hollow he began to come round to my way of thinking. When Jennifer joined me I became acutely aware of her femininity. As we crouched side by side with only a torch for illumination her hair brushed my face and her perfume briefly overpowered the smell of diesel. I struggled for a moment to remember where I'd got to in my explanation.

Once back on the ground I took them both into the workshop and showed them the packing material that I'd left arranged on the bench. It was easy to see that it formed four separate sections and that each section was approximately the same length as the stanchions in the engine compartment.

'What do those stanchions do?' Charlie asked.

'As far as I can tell they are meant to be extra support for the engine. I think the orginal engine was replaced at sometime by the existing one but I'm sure this newer one is bigger than the original.'

'But why are they hollow?'

'When the yacht left Auckland I think those stanchions were solid steel bars but the old man changed them during that stop in the islands. My theory is that he brought the tubing from Auckland, packed it with whatever he was smuggling, removed the steel bars and substituted the tubes.'

'That's why the packing material is asbestos,' exclaimed Jennifer. 'To protect whatever he was smuggling from the heat of the welding torch.'

'It's a great theory,' I said, 'but I can't prove a damn thing.'

Charlie looked thoughtful. 'You've almost convinced me,' he muttered.

'I'd better show you that second safe, there may be more clues in there if you can open it.'

'Do we need another combination?' Jennifer asked.

'No this time we need a key.' I pointed to the far corner of the room. 'It's over there.'

Jennifer walked over and crouched in front of the safe. 'I've seen a key somewhere. I'll have a look for it in the morning. At the moment I'm feeling extremely tired. I think my travelling is beginning to take its toll. Can we leave things as they are until tomorrow morning?'

'That's fine by me,' said Charlie. 'Just give me a ring when you're ready. I'll be in the office all day tomorrow.'

Jennifer turned to me, 'Terry?'

'Just call me,' I replied.

5

That evening I sat going over in my mind all that had happened since Jennifer Beddows had come into my life. Because of what we had discovered she had become quite a wealthy young woman. Had she realised it yet I wondered? She had said that her Grandfather was a secretive man, what other secrets did he have? There was still the second safe to open, the bank account in Fiji and of course the Kingston Islands.

I had an Ella Fitzgerald disc playing quietly in the background — I find that music helps my thought processes when I've got a puzzle to solve. This time the opposite happened instead of helping it began to mock me — Ella gave a beautiful rendition of the song 'I'm beginning to see the light'. That was one thing I wasn't seeing but what I could see however, was a strong possibility of overseas travel. I got up and checked that my passport was still valid.

Jennifer rang me just after ten the following morning and I was driving out of Beverley five minutes later. She said she had something to show me and she sounded quite excited. There were no preliminaries when I arrived at her place. She practically dragged me through the house, down the garden and into the workshop. On the workbench where I'd left the packing material lay an object covered with a cloth. She pointed to the cloth. 'Before I show what I've got here,' she said. 'I'd better explain that your idea of how Grandfather smuggled something into the country nagged at me until I had to do something about it. I had to know one way or the other.'

She then lifted the cloth and revealed a white plaster copy of the golden chess piece.

'How did you do that?' I exclaimed.

'It's plaster of Paris, I use it for modelling. Before I went to bed last night I came down here and examined this packing material.' She moved along the bench, pulled on a pair of rubber gloves and picked up a piece that was now spotted here and there with the white plaster. 'When I opened this piece the impression inside looked familiar so I decided to try using it as a mould. That she said,' pointing at the figure, 'is the result'.

'Can you do the same thing with rest of the packing?'

'I intend to,' she said with a smile. 'I'm waiting for some more plaster though. That was the last bit I had. I've just ordered some more it should arrive tomorrow.'

Picking up the plaster figure and examining it I noticed that it had a yellowish tinge in places. Pointing to it I asked what had caused the stain.

'Cooking oil,' she replied. 'I thought the plaster would probably stick to that material so I sprayed the packing with the oil first.'

'Good idea. Will you need help with the rest when the plaster arrives?'

She chuckled. 'It's messy work but if you're volunteering, then yes please.'

'Did you find the key for that other safe?'

'I haven't looked yet. There is a large brass key somewhere, I know there is but I can't remember where I've seen it.'

'I'm surprised you didn't know about that safe. It wasn't hidden it was just tucked away in the corner of the workshop.'

'Until you came on the scene I don't think anyone had been in here since Grandfather.'

'But he died six years ago.'

Jennifer nodded as she stripped off the rubber gloves. 'You think I've lived here all that time don't you?'

'I had assumed that, yes.'

'You're wrong. I suppose I'd better explain. Come on back to the house, I'll make some coffee and tell you about my last six years.'

Jennifer had left school at the age of eighteen with three good A-level passes and a guaranteed place at university. In common with many young people she'd decided to take a gap year, a year in which to recharge her batteries before facing that new challenge. She spent part of that year on the continent with a group of friends visiting Paris, Madrid, Barcelona and Venice. It was in Venice that the group began to split up and Jennifer decided to return home. For the next six months she worked as a shop assistant at a store in Hull. Although her parents had agreed to support her throughout her time at university she wanted financial independence and the wages she earned were carefully banked to that end.

In October 1999 Jennifer began her studies at Manchester University, English Literature with Art, a three-year degree course. However, in late November her Grandfather died and she returned home for the funeral and remained there over Christmas. She returned to University early in January in an attempt to catch up on the work she had missed but within days of her doing so she learnt of her parents' deaths.

At this point in her story Jennifer paused, blew her nose and wiped her eyes. 'I still can't believe it happened,' she said. 'Mother was only fifty. Dad was older, they married late.'

'What happened, can you tell me?' I asked.

'They were going shopping, the roads were icy and a lorry driver lost control on a bend. The lorry jack-knifed, skidded across the road and crushed their car against a tree. Dad died instantly and Mum died a few hours later in hospital.' She paused and wiped her eyes again. 'She died before I got there.'

'I'm sorry, I didn't mean to upset you,' I said.

'Sometimes when I look back at that period I feel as if it all happened to someone else. It's as if I was watching all that went on through a fog, as if I was watching another me sorting everything out.'

'Did you have any help?'

'Yes, of a sort. Grandfather's brother, Brian, came to do what he could but he was in the early stages of Altzheimers and was more of a hindrance than a help. Couple that with the fact that Mr Potts was almost senile then you can imagine what a mess it was.'

'What happened with the University?'

'Oh they were fine. I dropped out of my course that year and they let me restart in October 2000. By that time Mr Potts had sorted out my father's will but he'd put Grandfather's on hold while he did so.'

'You said your parents were going to support you through university. Did you manage okay financially?'

'I managed on my own money until probate was okayed on my father's will. After that I had their life insurance and the money from their bank accounts. Mind you I did have a problem because although I was at uni I had two houses to maintain, this one and my parent's place.'

'How on earth did you manage?'

'My parent's next door neighbours, Bill and Agnes Milburn, came to my rescue. They're retired now but at the time he was still working. They volunteered to look after the houses for me. Bill kept the gardens tidy and Agnes kept an eye on the insides. Once I'd got the finances straight I was able to employ them one day a week.'

'Have you still got both houses?'

'No I sold my parent's home. It had a

sizeable mortgage on it, draining my funds. I brought some of the furniture here though.'

'So how long have you actually lived here?'

'Just about two years. I got my degree in 2003 and came to live here shortly afterwards. Since then I've been fully employed with book illustrations.'

'Does that kind of work pay well?'

Jennifer chuckled. 'My agent assures me it will when I'm better known. At the moment I'm scraping along just about covering the bills.'

'Well you won't have to worry about bills anymore now that you've sorted out that Swiss account.'

'I haven't really. The money's okay, I've no problem with that. It's those stones that worry me. Where did he get them?' She suddenly stopped and snapped her fingers.

'That's it,' she exclaimed. 'I know where that key is.'

Jennifer stood up, chose a key from the rack and headed for the door. 'Come on, I've remembered where I've seen it.'

She led the way to the double garage at the side of the house, unlocked the door and switched on the light. I could see two cars, one of which I recognised as belonging to her. The other, an elderly Ford Escort was new to me. Pointing at the Escort Jennifer said, 'That was Grandfather's. I run the engine every now and again. It's my insurance policy, if mine breaks down I've always got that as a spare.'

Opening the door of the Escort she removed the keys from the ignition and showed them to me. Attached to the car keys was a brass coloured safe key. A few minutes later Jennifer opened the safe. There were three objects inside, an automatic pistol, a box of cartridges and a cardboard tube about thirty centimetres long. I cautiously removed the pistol and found that it was lightly oiled and fully loaded. It looked and felt ready for the business it was designed for. I replaced it. Jennifer meanwhile had opened the cardboard tube and removed a roll of paper from inside. She carefully spread it out on the bench and revealed a beautifully hand drawn map of the Kingston Islands.

'That's Grandfather's work, I'd recognise his handwriting anywhere,' she said. Turning back to the safe she visibly shuddered at the sight of the handgun. 'Lock that away again Terry, please lock it away.' Then taking the map she walked back towards the house.

6

Two days later the three of us met up again, this time in Charlie's office. Jennifer had requested the meeting and had brought with her not only the map of the islands but also the U.S. Navy document from the house safe. Charlie was on time for once. He opened the proceedings by detailing all that had happened in relation to the bank accounts that we had discovered. The Swiss account was now fully available for Jennifer to use. However, the account in Fiji required her presence with all the relevant documents before the funds there could be released. The bank had a branch in London which, under normal circumstances, could have dealt with the paperwork but once again there was a safety deposit box, this time in Fiji.

Once Charlie had finished, Jennifer took over. She produced the plaster model of the chess piece and told Charlie how she'd made it. Although she'd intended to make further models using the rest of the packing material, she hadn't been able to do so because her supplier of plaster of Paris had let her down. She was expecting a fresh delivery in about a week. Picking up the plaster model again, she spoke directly to Charlie.

'This more or less confirms Terry's theory of smuggling. I must confess to being very uneasy with what we've discovered over the past few days. First there was the smuggling theory, then the gemstones, this,' she said brandishing the model, 'and finally the gun.'

'Gun, what gun?' Charlie exclaimed.

'We found it a couple of days ago in that other safe. It's a German automatic and there's a box of cartridges as well,' I said.

Before Charlie could say anything Jennifer spoke again. 'I've been thinking hard about this whole business over the past couple of days and I must know more about my Grandfather's past. I want to formalise arrangements today for

Terry to investigate. I know it will probably mean him having to travel to these islands but if it's necessary I want it done.'

Charlie didn't say anything. He merely looked across at me and raised an eyebrow.

'Okay.' I said.

Jennifer sat back with a sigh of relief, Charlie muttered something about coffee and rang for Janice while I had my eye on the one document lying on the table that I hadn't had a chance to study. I leant across and picked it up. The heading was in bold black print — United States Navy Department, Pacific Command. It went on to detail the lease of Atoll 437, to be known for the duration of the lease as the Kingston Islands, and all the buildings thereon for a period of seventy-five years to the Auspac Marine Salvage Company. It was signed on behalf of the Auspac Company by Alfred Beddows, company secretary, and for the Navy Department by Commander Oswald D. Brubaker. A fee of two hundred U.S. dollars had been paid by the Auspac Salvage Company. It was dated June 1947. I passed it across to Charlie.

'Does that look legal?' I asked.

Charlie studied it for a few minutes. 'Yes, I think so. Have you got doubts?'

'Not doubts exactly. It's just that there was no mention of a lease when I queried this place with the U.S. Embassy.'

'I think you'd better check it out.'

'Now?'

'Yes, the sooner the better.'

Using the office phone I rang Stuart Gibson again and this time he was at his desk.

'Stuart it's Terry Jagger, I need some more help.'

'Is it the same problem?'

'Yes, Atoll 437. We've unearthed an official looking document that purports to be a lease for those islands. It's signed by a U.S. Navy commander and it's a seventy-five year lease to a marine salvage company.'

'That's odd, Jimmy never mentioned a lease.'

'Jimmy?'

'Yes he's my contact at the embassy

— James Footweller Junior, Lieutenant Commander, U.S. Navy.'

'Will you check it with him for me?'

'Sure, I'll ring you back.'

'Use my mobile number I'll probably be on the move. Oh, and thanks for the help, I really appreciate it.'

I was barely half way down my cup of coffee when Stuart rang back.

'Terry, you've got an appointment tomorrow at 1400 hours with Jimmy at the Embassy. He needs to see this lease you've found.'

'Thanks Stuart, pass on my regards to your family.'

'Will do, Christine sends her love by the way.' Once again he was laughing as he put down the phone.

As I slid my phone back into my pocket Charlie raised that questioning eyebrow of his again.

'The U.S. Embassy would like to see this,' I said, holding up the lease. 'I've got an appointment with the Naval Attaché in London tomorrow.'

'What time?'

'1400 hours.'

Charlie switched on the office inter-com. 'Janice, book Terry a seat on Hull Trains to London tomorrow. He has to be at the U.S. Embassy by 1400.'

Jennifer, who had been quietly sipping her coffee while Charlie and I had been busy with the various arrangements, got to her feet. 'Will you be travelling back tomorrow?' She asked.

'I hope so. I've no desire to spend a night in London.'

'Give me a ring when you get back, I can't wait to hear what the verdict is on that lease.'

'Before you go,' said Charlie looking at Jennifer. 'May I ask you to write down all that you know of your grandfather in order to give Terry a start and I also need to know when you're planning to go to Fiji.'

'I'll write Grandfather's details down today. As for Fiji, that depends on what Terry finds out tomorrow.'

I've heard all manner of moans about inefficiency, dirty carriages and late trains since the rail system was privatised but my journey to London the following day

67

was a revelation. Hull Trains provided an excellent service, clean and comfortable seating, pleasant courteous staff and an arrival at Kings Cross one minute ahead of time. I wish all forms of travel could be that good.

At the Embassy my passport and driving licence were carefully scrutinized, subjected to a computer check and returned to me after a wait of several minutes. Finally, I was escorted to the Naval Attaché's office by an armed marine where I was signed for like a parcel delivery. James Footweller Junior, Lieutenant Commander USN, was affability itself. His approach was immediately on first name terms.

'Terry,' he said shaking my hand, 'I've been hearing a lot about you from Stuart.'

'All good, I hope.'

'Naturally, now let's get down to business, coffee or tea?'

'Coffee please.'

He directed me to a comfortable leather armchair and seated himself opposite me a few minutes later. A uniformed orderly brought a tray of coffee and biscuits and then we got down to business.

'Tell me,' he said, 'why are you interested in Atoll 437?'

I began by explaining about Albert Beddows and the contents of his will and how in the course of investigating his overseas property we'd come across the lease document. He studied the document for a few minutes then asked for permission to photocopy it and after instructing his orderly to do the copying he opened a folder lying on the table in front of him.

'After Stuart first contacted me about this affair I had this file on the Atoll faxed from the U.S. records office. There is no record of any lease being agreed by the Navy Department.'

The orderly returned with the lease and and handed over a separate note at the same time. Jimmy studied the note.

'This document,' he said holding up the lease, 'is signed by a Commander Oswald D. Brubaker. The Navy List shows only one Oswald Brubaker. He was dishonourably discharged in 1918 and died shortly afterwards.'

'So the lease is a fake.' I said.

'Yes I'm afraid so. It appears that Alfred Beddows was the subject of a hoax and lost two hundred dollars in the process.'

'But he did make use of those islands.'

'That's true, but then anybody could after we left. Technically they are still Navy property but they are gradually disappearing into the sea so they're no use to us now.'

'Have you any idea what he was doing there?'

'No. Our inspection teams never found anyone there when they visited but they did find evidence of occupation. They also found this.'

He passed me a photograph. It was a picture of a grave and the inscription on the headstone read 'Valerie Beddows, R.I.P.'

'Good lord, that's the last thing I was expecting to see.'

'There was another grave, an unmarked one at the lower end of the island. That's gone now, it's underwater.'

I held up the photograph. 'Is this one still there?'

He nodded. 'It was five years ago at the last inspection.'

'What do these teams inspect?'

'The state of the anchorage mainly, it's still a safe harbour in rough weather for vessels up to around six thousand tons.'

'Do I need permission to land there?'

'Are you planning to go?'

'My client, Miss Beddows may want me to when I tell her about this.' I held up the photograph. 'May I keep this copy?'

'Yes, I had that run off for you. As for permission to land, that won't be necessary. However, I'd appreciate it if you'd inform me if you do decide to go.'

'How does one get there?'

'By sea nowadays, the runway has virtually disappeared and even when it was new it wasn't much good.'

'Why not?'

'It was put there as an emergency strip for carrier based aircraft. Because of its short length they had to install arrestor wires like those on a carrier.'

'Could they take off again?'

'Only the small stuff could and then

only if they were lightly laden. Anything bigger was taken out by sea. They blew a hole in the reef to let bigger ships in for that purpose.'

'I can see now why it was abandoned so soon after the war.'

'Yes, it was useless once jets came in.'

We parted company shortly afterwards with promises on my part to keep in touch if it was decided necessary to visit the atoll. The embassy car delivered me to King's Cross in time to catch the four o'clock train. I was driving home just after eight that evening.

Throughout that journey I agonised on how to break the news to Jennifer about her Grandmother's grave. I even began to wonder whether it was Jennifer's grandmother or some other member of the family I knew nothing of. In the end I decided to play it by ear and hope for the best. Instead of stopping at my place I continued on to Jennifer's. If she was surprised by my arrival she didn't show it when she answered the door.

'I thought at first you must be someone electioneering but then I recognised the car. Come in, would you like a coffee or something stronger?'

'Coffee would be fine, thanks.'

We walked through into the kitchen and I immediately thought I was beginning to see more of that room than the one in my own home. Jennifer must have had similar thoughts because as I sat down and she poured the coffee she smiled and said, 'I see you've taken a liking to that chair.'

'It's comfortable,' I replied.

'It was Grandfather's favourite,' she said as she sat opposite me. 'Now, what did you learn today?'

'Apparently the lease is a fake. The U.S. Navy department has no record of it and the man whose signature appears on it died in 1918.'

'So what was Grandfather doing there?'

'I don't know and neither does the U.S. Navy. However I do have a serious question for you. Who was Valerie Beddows?'

She looked puzzled. 'I've no idea,' she said, 'I've never heard of her. Why do you ask?'

73

I handed her the photograph of the gravestone. 'That was taken by a Navy photographer on those islands. Was she your grandmother?'

'Definitely not. My Grandmother's name was Elizabeth. She was killed during the blitz on Hull in 1941. Grandfather was very secretive but I do know about Elizabeth. Father told me that.'

She sat studying the photograph for some minutes before speaking again. 'We've got to go there, we must find out what he was doing.'

'We?' I said.

'Yes, I've been thinking things over. I've got to go to Fiji so I might as well go the whole hog. How do we get there?'

I suppressed a yawn then got to my feet. 'Let's leave that until tomorrow Jennifer. I'd better get home before I fall asleep in your chair.'

She walked with me to the door. 'Jenny,' she said. 'My friends call me Jenny.'

7

I slept badly that night, my sleep interrupted by dreams in which boats, planes and guns seemed to feature quite a bit. Jennifer appeared in one particular episode because I distinctly remembered her repeating the phrase 'my friends call me Jenny'. I woke about three o'clock disturbed by my unconscious thoughts but apart from the boats and planes etc I couldn't remember what the dreams were about. Wandering through to the kitchen I switched on the kettle with the intention of making a hot drink. When the water boiled I decided that the caffeine in tea or coffee wouldn't help my sleep problem so, instead, I poured myself a brandy. I don't think that helped either but it did warm me up. I finally got back to sleep about four thirty Friday morning.

Friday, named after Freya, goddess of love and the night, would she look kindly on me that day I wondered. Despite my poor night's sleep I was still up and about before the postman arrived. Mind you that doesn't mean much nowadays. My mail used to be delivered before nine every morning but now it can be anytime between eight and midday. That day two offers for credit cards, three for car insurance and one for a catalogue I hadn't ordered, all found their way rather rapidly into the recycling bin. Twenty minutes later, having breakfasted on tea and toast, I was on my way to Charlie's office.

Charlie was busy with a client when I arrived so I spent some time with his secretary Janice. Together we began the process of tracing Albert Beddows past. I gave Janice a list of the various birth, marriage and death certificates of the Beddows family that I felt might be useful in tracking Albert's past. Despite Jennifer's assertion that she'd never heard of Valerie Beddows I added her name to the list. By the time we'd completed that and got the requests off in the post Charlie's client had finished his business. He didn't seem too happy about it though as he slammed his way out of the office. Charlie emerged a few minutes later and handed a cheque to Janice.

'Post it to him Janice then close the file, he won't be back here.'

'Did you upset him Charlie?' I asked.

'I didn't, that was his late father's doing.'

'I shouldn't ask, should I?'

'You don't have to, that was David Harrison. His affairs were headline news in the local paper a few days ago.'

'Oh, I remember, his father left his fortune to an animal rescue centre.'

'That's the one. The old man hadn't seen David for nearly twenty years despite the fact they only lived a few miles apart.'

'Wasn't there something about bus fares?' I said.

'That's it,' said Charlie pointing to the cheque. 'His father left him ten pounds to attend the funeral, he didn't even manage that. Now he wants me to contest the will.'

'I take it you've turned him down.'

Charlie nodded. 'I liked the old man. He was very independent despite being stuck in a wheelchair for the last twenty years of his life.'

'Why?'

'Skiing accident, he crushed a couple of vertebrae.'

'No, I meant, why did you like him?'

'Oh I see. I liked him because despite his injuries he refused to give up. He continued to run the business until a couple of years ago. He liked his drink, loved life, was a great raconteur and the ladies adored him. I even had to defend him once for being drunk in charge of a wheelchair.'

'He sounds like my kind of man,' I said.

'I'm not surprised, like you he was in the Navy.'

'When?'

'During the Second World War, he was a 'hostilities only' officer, Lieutenant RNVR.'

'That's the third time that war has been mentioned in the last twenty-four hours.'

'Who by?' Charlie asked.

'Well the first to bring it up was the American, Jimmy Footweller, then Jenny last night and now you.'

'You saw Miss Beddows last night?'

'I had to. I couldn't telephone her with this.' I handed Charlie the photograph of the gravestone.

'Valerie Beddows,' said Charlie reading the inscription. 'Who is she?'

I spent another fifteen minutes going over all that I had learned the previous day from both the Americans and from Jennifer. Charlie was surprised to learn that Jennifer had decided to travel not only to Fiji but also on to the Kingston Islands with me. However, he wasn't surprised to learn that the lease on the islands was a fake. I went on to tell him about the work Janice and I had initiated that morning while he'd been busy with the Harrison affair. When I finally finished he picked up the photograph again.

'Miss Beddows doesn't know of this member of the family.'

'No, she says it's definitely not her Grandmother, she was killed in 1941 and her name was Elizabeth.'

'A second wife?' Charlie mused.

'It's possible, but why didn't the family know about her?'

Charlie looked up at me and a slow smile spread across his face. 'That's your job,' he said. 'That's what you've been hired to find out.'

'Jenny mentioned Albert's brother the other day, do you know if he's still alive?'

'Jenny?'

'Jenny to me, Miss Beddows to you Charlie. Well is he still alive?'

'I've no idea, you'll have to ask Miss Beddows,' he replied with a hint of sarcasm in his voice. 'You'll have to watch yourself Terry, eligible bachelor like you escorting a young beauty like her to the South Pacific. She'll have you walking down the aisle in no time at all.'

'That's not a bad idea, Charlie,' I said as I got up and made for the door. I glanced back and he was sitting there with his mouth open.

A few minutes later I drove into the car park at the new medical centre in Woodhall Way. I knew that in travelling to the South Pacific I would require certain vaccinations and a prescription for anti-malaria tablets. Half an hour later I left with a sore arm and a packet of tablets. I'd just happened to arrive at the centre when my doctor had some spare time slots — one 'no show' and one cancellation allowed me to be dealt with immediately. That had never happened to me before.

Before I left the car park I rang Jennifer. She told me that not only was Brian Beddows, Albert's brother, still alive but his wife Brenda was as well. The pair of them were living in a residential care home in Bridlington. We made arrangements to drive out to Bridlington together that afternoon.

Jennifer had warned me not to expect too much from Brian Beddows, her great uncle, but I still wasn't prepared for what we found. He was sitting at a table assembling a child's Meccano set with a plastic spanner. Jennifer spoke to him but he ignored her and carried on working away with his simple tool.

'He doesn't know you're there,' said a quiet voice from behind us. 'He doesn't know I'm here and we've been married sixty odd years.'

I turned to face the speaker and as I did so Jennifer brushed past me and kissed the old lady who'd come up behind us. She was seated in a wheel chair and looked so frail that I estimated that anything stronger than a stiff breeze would blow her away. She offered her left hand to me as Jennifer introduced us, her right hand lay immobile in her lap.

'Ironic, isn't it,' she said. 'His body's in good nick but his mind's gone. I've still got most of my marbles but everything else is crumbling away.'

'What is he building?' I asked.

'Only he knows. He just fastens everything together in no particular order then sits and looks at it. Eventually one of the assistants will come along and dismantle it then he'll start assembling again.'

Jennifer took over the conversation for a short while asking how her aunt was and explaining the purpose of our visit. When Jennifer produced the photograph of the grave on the islands Brenda looked at it in silence for some time before finally admitting that she'd never heard of Valerie Beddows.

'Albert was badly affected by the war,' she said. 'He was at sea when Elizabeth was killed and he didn't know she was dead until he got back three months later.'

'Was he in the Navy?' I asked.

'He was an engineer in the Merchant Navy. He served his apprenticeship with one of the ship repair companies on Hedon Road in Hull. As soon as he qualified he went off to sea.'

'When did Elizabeth die?' Jennifer asked.

'In the blitz, May 1941, I think it was the night of the ninth. There were hundreds killed that night.'

'My father survived,' said Jennifer

'Yes, that was something of a miracle. He was in his pram under the staircase. The rescue teams found him the next morning covered in plaster dust and very hungry. His cries lead them to him.'

'How old was he?' I asked.

'Six weeks old and seven pounds in

weight, I became his mother then.'

Jennifer placed her hand on the old lady's shoulder. 'I've always wondered,' she said, 'if you actually adopted father.'

'Not officially, because of his name everyone assumed I was his mother. Albert helped financially and he sent us food parcels for a number of years after the war.'

'You said that Albert was badly affected by the war. Do you mean by Elizabeth's death?' I interjected.

'By that and by the Russian convoys, he sailed on three of those but refused to go on any more after PQ17.'

'He survived that did he?'

The old lady nodded. 'He came back looking like death warmed up,' she said. 'His ship was torpedoed and he spent days in an open boat. The Russian doctors had to amputate some of his toes because of frostbite.'

'He went back to sea though, didn't he?' Jennifer asked.

'Oh yes. He stayed with us for two weeks after he came back from Russia. He'd sit by the fire staring into it for hours not saying a word. I thought he was losing his mind then suddenly one day he got up, packed his gear and went.'

'Did he say goodbye?'

'He kissed the baby, gave me a hug and said, 'He's yours now Brenda'. The next time we saw him the war was over.'

The three of us sat and talked for another quarter of an hour. There wasn't much more she could tell us about Albert because apart from a couple of short visits in the years immediately after the war they saw nothing of him until he bought the house in Little Driffield. Shortly afterwards we took our leave with Jennifer promising to pay another visit before we left for Fiji.

In the car on the journey back I was deep in thought until Jennifer spoke.

'What was PQ17?'

'An unmitigated disaster,' I replied. 'It was a massive convoy of about fifty merchant ships escorted by a number of warships. The merchant ships were carrying guns, tanks, planes, and everything else it takes to fight a war, to Russia.'

'What happened?'

'The Admiralty ordered the warships to leave the convoy and the convoy to scatter. The result was that only a handful of the merchant ships reached Russia the rest were sunk by German submarines and aircraft.'

'Why was that order given?'

'The Admiralty received information that a large fleet of German warships were sailing to attack the convoy. By the time they realised that the information was wrong the convoy had been destroyed.'

'I can understand why Grandfather refused to go to Russia again.'

'So can I,' I said. 'There are still a few survivors who blame the Royal Navy for that shambles.'

8

Jenny had a painting commission to complete so there was no question of us heading off to Fiji immediately. This gave me time to contact Fiji's yacht club to obtain details of yachts available for charter. There was no other way we could reach the Kingston Islands, aircraft couldn't land, they were too remote for helicopters to reach them and there was no regular shipping passing that way. It had to be a yacht charter if we were to get there at all.

While I was waiting for a response from Fiji the various birth, marriage and death certificates of the Beddows family arrived in dribs and drabs. There was no record of Valerie Beddows whatsoever. As far as the British registration system was concerned she had never existed. That probably meant that she had been the citizen of another country but which one I wondered. Albert had named his yacht

Island Beauty, was Valerie the island beauty in question?

As far as the yacht was concerned things were put on hold. Jennifer decided to leave things as they were until we'd paid our visit to the South Pacific. I did spend a day finishing off the tidying up that I'd started some days earlier before finally replacing the tarpaulins and making everything secure once again. Despite my best efforts to make the tarpaulins as tight as possible they still sagged in places, allowing rainwater to accumulate in small pools. Two days later when Jennifer and I made our way down to the workshop there was a blackbird happily bathing in one of them.

Our efforts with the plaster of Paris when it finally turned up proved largely inconclusive. The plaster models we produced were nowhere near as clearly defined as the chess piece. The results were long, thin, sausage shaped objects that gave very little indication of what they contained. There were two, however, that could have held coins because there were faint indications of milled edges. I experimented with a hundred small pebbles that I collected from the driveway. Wrapping them in cling film in sections approximately the same size as the plaster casts I laid them out alongside each other. The match was almost perfect. Jennifer had said there were approximately one hundred gemstones in the safe deposit box in Switzerland and my pebbles matched them. As for the two that could have held coins I tried pound coins for size but they proved to be smaller than the supposedly smuggled ones. If they were coins most were larger than a pound but smaller than a ten pence piece.

That particular day, the day of the gem and coin experiments, I drove home with something indefinable niggling away at the back of my mind. Something I'd done that day had triggered a background thought process that was still troubling me when I went to bed. It was two o'clock in the morning when I suddenly sat up. I'd remembered what it was. What I'd seen was a crumpled receipt in Albert's desk back on day one when I'd been searching for the safe combination. A receipt from a coin dealer.

Despite my early morning awakening I did get a good night's sleep. I telephoned Jennifer before nine o'clock that morning and asked her to check that the receipt was not a figment of my imagination.

'I've found it,' she said. 'It's from a coin dealer called Phillips with an address in York.'

'Thank goodness it wasn't my memory playing tricks on me,' I replied. 'I think I'll drive into York this morning and have a chat with Mr Phillips.'

'Do you want some company?'

'I'd love some. When shall I pick you up?'

'Give me twenty minutes, I'm still in my dressing gown,' she answered.

I remember almost making a facetious remark about my helping her out of it but I managed to control myself. I merely remarked that I'd be there on time.

The weather was fine when we drove away from the house but as we drove west towards York the skies began to darken. There were flashes of lightning and low rumbles of thunder but the rain didn't start until we were approaching Garrowby Hill. By the time we began the descent of what can be an extremely dangerous gradient the rain was lashing down. I had the windscreen wipers on full power but they were unable to cope with the deluge so I pulled off the road into a small lay-by. As I brought the car to a halt the storm broke directly above us. There was a tremendous crash of thunder that literally shook the car and forked lightning cracked to earth a short distance ahead of us. Jennifer gripped my hand. We sat there holding hands for fully fifteen minutes whilst the storm raged around us. The thunder made talking impossible so we sat and watched nature's firework display without saying a word.

As the storm began to move away Jennifer's grip on my hand relaxed, however, she didn't release her hold altogether. Outside the rain had lessened but there was still a river of rainwater running down the hill so I decided to wait until the rain stopped. As we watched the sun broke through the cloud and lit up the Vale of York below us. A rainbow appeared and the landscape began to glow. Every second field appeared to be bright gold, it was a brilliant patchwork of colour as far as the eye could see. Oilseed rape seemed to be taking over the countryside. It was interspersed with fields of various shades of green and brown.

Jennifer broke the spell by releasing her grip on my hand. She pointed to the valley below. 'The Irish have a song about forty shades of green. They're not the only ones are they?'

'At this time of year every tree and hedge seems to be a different shade,' I replied as I started the engine and drove out onto the road.

Fifteen minutes later we were standing outside a small, old fashioned looking jewellery shop. The sign above the shop read 'J. Phillips and Son Jewellers and Coin Dealers'. I pressed the buzzer by the door and a young man behind the counter looked up, pushed a button by his side and the door swung open. As we entered the shop there was a quiet hissing sound behind us followed by a loud clunk. We were in and from the sound of that clunk, locked in. A second man emerged from a door at the rear, he was older, probably in his mid forties. I addressed the younger man.

'May we have a word with Mr Phillips?'

It was the older of the two that replied. 'I'm John Phillips,' he said. 'How may I help you?'

I introduced Jennifer and myself and showed him the receipt we'd found. The receipt merely stated that the jeweller had purchased goods to the value of several hundred pounds from Albert Beddows but it did not specify what the goods were. I explained that I represented a firm of solicitors and that we were attempting to finalise Albert Beddows affairs. It was then that I introduced a little white lie into the conversation.

'Mr Beddow's will specified a number of items which included jewellery and coins. Unfortunately we've been unable to find some of these items. The will was made some time before he died and he may well have sold some of those items and forgotten to change his will. We'd like to know what this receipt represents.'

'This is extremely irregular,' he replied. 'However, I am prepared to consider your request if you have proof of your story.'

He wanted to see the will but of course I deliberately didn't have a copy to show him. Jennifer produced her Grandfather's death certificate and her passport whilst I showed my driving licence. I then persuaded him to ring Charlie's office to seek confirmation of our story. He even looked up the office number in his telephone directory to make sure I wasn't trying to con him with a phoney number. Eventually he was satisfied and led us through to the back of the shop.

'My father dealt with Mr Beddows, that's his signature on the receipt.' He sat at a desk and tapped away at a computer keyboard before continuing. 'He retired four years ago and I've computerised all his records since then.'

'So you never met my Grandfather,' said Jennifer.

'I can't remember doing so,' he replied.

'Ah, here we are, Albert Beddows. Four transactions between 1997 and 1999, all gold coins in mint condition. I can't be anymore precise than that. No, hang on a minute there's a fifth purchase, a very old one. December 1949, diamonds to the value of over one thousand pounds.'

'When?' I exclaimed.

'December 1949, they must have been excellent quality for father to part with that sort of money back then.'

'Is your father still alive?' I asked.

'Very much so but he lives abroad now. I could ask him if he remembers any more details when I next speak to him if you like.'

'That would be a great help, thank you.' I gave him my card. 'Would you mind sending details to the office if you can't contact me, I may well be out of the country following up further details of Mr Beddow's will.'

He nodded agreement and both Jennifer and I thanked him for his help. As the shop door closed behind us with that resounding clunk Jennifer took my hand. We walked a few paces down the street before she stopped and turned towards me. She stood gazing into my face for fully half a minute before speaking. 'How do you do it?' she asked.

'Do what?'

'Tell lies without turning a hair.'

'It was only a little white lie and it got us a result,' I protested.

She laughed and squeezed my hand. 'I'm only jealous,' she said. 'I could never keep a straight face if I had to do it.'

'The first time I told one was when I was in the Navy. I was a watchkeeping officer in a frigate and we got caught in a typhoon in the South China Sea.'

'Go on,' prompted Jennifer. 'Don't keep me in suspense.'

'I'd never seen weather so bad and to be honest I was decidedly worried about our chances of survival. Virtually everything that could be swept overboard had gone and that included most of our liferafts. There were six of us in the wheelhouse and everyone except the captain was sick.'

'You as well?'

'Oh yes, I was very seasick. There was a

young signalman on watch with me and we were sharing the same bucket to be sick in. He was terrified and he showed it. The wind was screaming so you had to shout to be heard and he shouted to me and asked if we were going to survive.'

'What did you say?'

'I looked him straight in the eyes and shouted back, 'of course we will, this ship was built to come through weather like this. It'll be rough for a while but we'll be okay.' I think he believed me.'

I remember I burst into laughter then.

'What are you laughing about?' Jennifer asked.

'It was what happened a few minutes later. The captain tapped me on the shoulder and shouted in my ear. He said, 'Thank you for those words of encouragement Jagger, I was beginning to doubt whether we'd survive this lot myself.' '

'Was anybody hurt?'

'There were several men with broken bones, a couple had burns and one man had a heart attack but they all survived.'

'What happened to the ship?'

'After three weeks of dockyard mainte-
nance in Singapore she was as good as
new. Come on, that's enough about my
past, I'll buy you a coffee before we head
for home.'

9

For almost a week after our trip to York I remained kicking my heels at home. Jennifer had completed her latest project but was waiting for her publisher to confirm that the work was satisfactory. Our only contact during that period was by telephone. We were both ready to leave for Fiji the minute her clearance came through. The only thing left for us to do was to confirm our date of departure with the travel agents.

I'd received details from the Royal Yacht Club in Fiji of three yachts that were available for charter and all of them were berthed in Suva harbour. Of the three the one I liked the sound of best was similar in construction to *Island Beauty*, a yacht built for serious ocean cruising rather than a weekend gin palace. She came with a local skipper and from my point of view that was extremely useful since Jennifer had no sailing experience whatsoever.

My boredom was relieved on the Thursday morning when I received a phone call from John Phillips, the coin dealer in York.

'Mr Jagger, it's John Phillips, I've just spoken to my father. He's visiting friends in Amsterdam but he'll be flying to Malta tomorrow. He's willing to meet you at Schipol Airport in the morning.'

'I'll have to check flight times, when will he be there?'

'He's prepared to meet the early morning flight from Humberside. It leaves at half past six. Shall I tell him you'll be on it?'

'If there's a seat available I'll be on it.'

'There is, he's already checked.'

'How will I recognise him?'

'He's five feet six, has a small moustache and he always wears a navy blue pin stripe suit when he's travelling. I've given him a description of you as well.'

'Tell him I'll be there and thank you for arranging the meeting.'

I rang Charlie's office to put him in the

picture. Charlie had a case in court that day so I left a message with his secretary. She booked my flight for me and arranged for me to pick up the tickets from the airport the following day. When I telephoned Jennifer the only response I got was from her answering machine so once again I had to leave a message. She did ring me back however, about an hour later. Neither of us was quite certain what we could gain from the meeting but I had a feeling that old Mr Phillips had something to tell us, something he wasn't prepared to say on the telephone.

For once it was a pleasure to drive to the airport. The sun was just beginning to colour the sky, the roads were empty and the air it felt pleasantly warm. I had two encounters with rabbits and one with a hedgehog but they all survived. Crossing the Humber Bridge I could see that the river had that liquid chocolate look that I associate with the Humber estuary on calm days.

When I boarded the aircraft I found

myself seated across the aisle from a pale-faced woman wearing a headscarf. Shortly after we had taken-off the lady in question began the transformation from pale-faced waif to authoritative business-woman. The first stage was the removal of the headscarf and the twenty or so plastic hair curlers it concealed. That was swiftly followed by the application of a small hairbrush. Once she was satisfied with her hair she turned her attention to her makeup. This was very carefully applied — any slight movement of the aircraft caused her to suspend operations until the machine steadied again. We were on the approach to Schipol when she finally patted her hair one last time, folded her mirror away and gave me a gleaming smile. The transformation was amazing. I'd brought a book to read and instead had watched a fascinating chapter in life's rich pattern.

The senior member of the Phillips family was there to meet me as arranged. After we had settled at one of the tables in the main body of the terminal with coffee and toast for breakfast the old man was the first to speak.

'What do you want to know about Alfred Beddows?'

'Everything you know about him. I'm representing his granddaughter and there are all manner of questions we need answers to, for instance when did you first meet him?'

'That's easy enough, late in 1949. I was still trying to establish my jewellery business when he walked in through the door with some of the most perfect diamonds I'd ever seen. There were two flawless yellows that had me drooling.'

'Was that it, two diamonds?'

'Oh no, there were eight altogether. The rest were blue-white, again virtually flawless. I had to borrow from the bank to buy them.'

'Did you ask him where he got them?'

'I did but he wouldn't tell me. There were all sorts of exchange controls at that time. There were limits on financial movements in and out of the country and I was almost certain he'd brought them in illegally.'

'Why were you so certain?'

'The way he carried them. Do you remember the double-ended Swan Vesta match boxes?'

'Yes,' I replied, rather puzzled by the question.

'He'd adapted one. One quarter held matches and the remainder held the diamonds packed in cottonwool.'

'Crafty old bugger,' I said.

'No, he wasn't old then. This was just after the war, fifty-odd years ago.'

'What did you think when he came back all those years later with the coins?'

'I must admit I was suspicious at first. The sovereigns he had were so perfect that they looked as if they'd just been minted. I only bought a few from him the first time and I had one of them assayed. It was okay though so after that I bought whatever he brought.'

'Were they all sovereigns?'

'No, there were a few Austrian coins and even some Russian ones.'

'I don't suppose he said where he got them?'

'No, he was as tight lipped as ever but

some of them had tiny salt crystals stuck to them.'

'Salt! Well he was a seaman. I'm supposed to trace his background and apart from the fact that he worked in the South Pacific I know virtually nothing about him.'

'There was one other thing,' muttered the old jeweller. 'I don't know if it's relevant but some of the stones almost certainly came from the Indian sub-continent. The man who cut and polished them was thought to be a Portugese living in Goa.'

'You could tell that from looking at them,' I exclaimed.

'I couldn't, not at that time, but the man I sold them to could. He was a real diamond expert.'

'There are more,' I said.

I watched his eyes light up. 'Where?' He gasped.

'In Switzerland.'

'Are they for sale?'

'They could be, but not at the moment.'

'I'd like to be given first refusal,' he

said, handing me a business card. 'I'm supposed to be retired but I'm still interested in stones, particularly dia-monds.'

The card showed an address in Malta. 'That's my home address,' he said as he glanced at his watch. He got to his feet. 'I'll have to go, my flight leaves shortly.'

We shook hands and he hurried away. I watched him until he turned towards his departure gate and disappeared from view, a jaunty little man in a pin-striped suit carrying a KLM flight bag. Would I be seeing him again in the near future I wondered?

During my flight back to Humberside airport I went over in my mind all that I had learned from the old jeweller. He was certain that some of the stones he'd bought in 1949 had originated in India. From the little I knew of Albert Beddows there was no indication of him ever visiting that country. However, there was a link with India in the South Pacific. The islands of Fiji had a large Indian population. They had originally been brought to Fiji in the nineteenth century

106

by our colonial forebears to work the extensive sugar cane plantations but over the years their descendants had moved up through the social strata. There were Fijian born Indians in virtually every profession now including senior politicians. Albert had a bank account in Fiji, had he been trading with a jeweller there?

The following morning the three of us met again at Charlie's office. Charlie began the proceedings by producing all the various birth, marriage and death certificates I'd asked for. They confirmed everything we already knew about the Beddows family but once again there was no record of a Valerie Beddows. After Charlie had finished it fell to me to go over all that I had learned from Mr Phillips. Finally it was Jennifer's turn and she introduced a surprise element into the meeting.

'I know the significance of that diamond sale in 1949,' she said.

'You do!' Charlie exclaimed.

She nodded. 'I visited Aunt Brenda yesterday and she was rather more forthcoming about events just after the war. She'd obviously had time to think things over since our last visit.'

'So what was the significance?'

'He sold the diamonds to give Brian and Brenda money for my father's education. Apparently he still felt he had to support the child even though he'd virtually given him to Brenda.'

'Was that all you learned?' I asked.

'No, for some years after that he sent food parcels and sometimes lengths of material to be made up into clothing. Apparently food and clothing were still rationed in this country until well into the 1950s.'

'Did she say where the parcels came from?'

'Yes, New Zealand, Singapore, Australia and she remembered at least two were from South Africa.'

'Wasn't there anything from Fiji?'

'She did mention one parcel from there, four pounds of coarse brown sugar. It arrived in time for Christmas one year. She swopped some of the sugar for raisins and was able to make a Christmas cake for the first time since the war had ended.'

'That reminds me of my parents,' said Charlie. 'They used to grow vegetables in the garden and swop with their neighbours. You know the sort of thing — your four carrots for my two onions.'

'It's a pity that it doesn't happen nowadays,' replied Jennifer. 'It would certainly make the likes of Tesco sit up and take notice. I personally wish the farmer's market at Driffield showground was once a week instead of once a month.'

'Whoa,' I interrupted. 'Aren't we wandering away from the point here, is there anything more of relevance to say?'

'Yes,' said Jennifer. 'When can we leave?'

'Leave?'

'For Fiji.'

'Is your publisher satisfied with your work then?'

'She's not only satisfied, she's given me a new commission to work on while we're away. Parrots and palm trees and such.'

Charlie leaned forward and switched on the intercom. 'Janice,' he said. 'Get the travel agents on the phone, these two are leaving us in the very near future.'

10

For me long distance air travel is
something to be endured rather than
enjoyed. Suffice to say that after flying
from Leeds/Bradford airport to London
we joined an Air New Zealand flight to
Fiji via Los Angeles. There were only two
good things of note about that journey.
One, we travelled in the relative comfort
of business class and two, Jennifer was
sitting beside me. Sometime the following
day we stumbled off the aircraft and into
Nandi airport in Fiji. We were both
suffering from lack of sleep and thoroughly disorientated by our crossing of
the international-date-line. We booked
into the nearest airport hotel and slept
the clock around.

Nandi (spelt Nadi but pronounced
Nandi) is on the main Fijian island of Viti
Levu. The port of Suva is at the opposite
side of that island. Both the bank that
Jennifer had to visit and the yachts that I

wanted to inspect were in Suva. There were two ways of getting there from Nandi, a half-hour flight or a half-day drive. We opted for the flight to Nausori, Suva's airport, and the twenty-minute taxi ride to the Travelodge Hotel.

Apart from making appointments by telephone for the following day we did nothing more by way of business. Instead we strolled along Victoria Parade getting our bearings and soaking up the atmosphere. Jennifer remarked on the brilliant colours of the bougainvillea and hibiscus and of the heady scent of frangipani. She was fascinated by the colourful attire of the people and by the racial variety. There were Fijian men in sulus and their womenfolk in dresses that ranged in style from Victorian England to modern day Paris and Indian ladies in brilliantly coloured saris. Chinese traders, Australasian, American and Japanese tourists all added to the cosmopolitan mix. We investigated an open market where amongst the exotica on display were pineapples, papaya, mangoes and guava. There were children sucking on sticks of sugar cane and everywhere we went people greeted us with smiles.

Later, back at the hotel, I decided to take a dip in the pool in order to cool down. Jennifer followed my example but by the time she arrived at the poolside I'd had a swim and had ordered fruit cocktails for both of us. However, the sight of Jennifer in a bikini ruined my efforts to cool down and I had to return to the pool for a while. Even later when we had dinner together I had to give myself a mental kick more than once to remind me that there was a serious side to our visit to Fiji rather than a romantic holiday. We dined at a table overlooking the moonlit harbour and the combination of that view, the warmth, and the tropical smells and sounds had a mesmerising and relaxing effect. At that moment in time I could have cheerfully joined the lotus-eaters of the modern world.

The following morning we got down to serious business. We had an appointment at the bank for eleven o'clock but before that we were hoping to view the first of the yachts available for charter. It was berthed a few minutes drive outside Suva in the Bay of Islands. We found the boat quickly enough but rousing its Australian skipper took us rather longer. When he eventually came up on deck I knew at once that we'd found one of today's lotus-eaters. Initially only his head and shoulders appeared out of the fore hatch. His matted blonde hair stuck out in all directions, his eyes told a tale of late nights and plenty of booze whilst his chin hadn't seen a razor for several days. Seeing us he mumbled, 'I'll just get me kecks on', before disappearing down the hatch again. A few minutes later he reappeared in the cockpit wearing the tattiest pair of shorts I'd ever seen and nothing else.

'G'day sport,' he said. His eyes rested briefly on me then switched rapidly to take in Jennifer's attributes. He reluctantly dragged his eyes back to me when I asked permission to come aboard.

'Sure,' he said. 'Fancy a tinny?' He held up the can of beer that he was drinking from to illustrate his question.

As I was helping Jennifer aboard two

young island girls climbed out of the fore hatch and dived into the clear waters of the bay. They were both wearing the briefest of brief bikinis. 'Great girls,' he said. He turned to us again and with a leer at Jennifer asked, 'What can I do you for?'

'The charter,' I replied.

'Ah, pity that,' he said, scratching his chin as he did so.

'Pity?'

'Aye, I've got the girls aboard for two of my mates from Oz. They want a trip round the islands.'

'Does that mean you're not available for charter?'

'Probably,' he said. 'Although I might be able to take you on in about three or four weeks time.'

He shook the beer can he was holding then turned and went below again, presumably to find a fresh one. I moved across to the companionway to call down to him and was met by a waft of stale air from below, air that reeked of beer, cigarettes and last night's sex.

'We'll be on our way then,' I called.

'Okay, be seeing you sport.'

A few minutes later, as we began the short walk back to the hotel, he reappeared out of the fore hatch. This time we could clearly see that as he joined the girls in the water he was completely naked.

'If he'd worn his shorts he might have washed some of the dirt out of them,' observed Jennifer.

'They'd have probably disintegrated altogether,' I replied.

Our visit to the bank was much more successful. We were greeted by the manager, Mr Patel, escorted to a private room and supplied with coffee and biscuits before he would even discuss business. The three of us drank coffee and talked small talk for fully fifteen minutes before Jennifer was able to bring the conversation round to her Grandfather.

'Did you ever meet my Grandfather, Mr Patel?'

'Oh yes, we were on first name terms. He dined at my home several times.'

'What did he do out here?'

Mr Patel held up his hand. 'This morning is for business but tonight I will tell you all I know about Albert. Will you both join me for dinner at my home?'

Jennifer glanced across at me and I gave a small nod. 'Thank you,' she said. 'We'd love to come.'

'My car will collect you from the Travelodge at seven-thirty if that is satisfactory.'

'Yes, of course but we didn't say which hotel we were staying at.'

Mr Patel gave a slight smile. 'Miss Beddows,' he said. 'Suva may be Fiji's capital but it is relatively small. It has a jungle telegraph system that is second to none. I knew you were in town five minutes after you signed the hotel register.' He pressed a button on the wall by his chair. 'Now to business,' he said.

The door opened and a younger man entered the room. 'May I introduce my son, Himat, he is here to attend to the paperwork. Do you have it with you?'

Jennifer opened her handbag and passed an envelope to him. Opening it he handed each item separately to his son after first checking it himself. 'Miss Beddow's passport, her birth certificate, Albert Beddow's death certificate and a copy of his will and finally a copy of the death certificate of David Beddows.' After handing these over to his son he turned back to Jennifer. 'Did you bring the key to the safe deposit box?'

Jennifer took a key from her bag. 'Is this it?' She asked.

Taking it from her he turned it over in his hand before handing it back. 'Yes,' he replied. 'That is one of our keys.' He got to his feet. 'If you would like to remain here for a few minutes whilst Himat deals with the paperwork I'll get someone to escort you down to the safe deposit area.'

It was ten minutes later when Himat reappeared bringing with him several sheets of paper for Jennifer's attention. I got to my feet. 'I'll wait outside,' I said.

'I'd like you to stay,' said Jennifer. 'You are after all my solicitor's assistant. I may need your help.'

I sat down again and listened carefully

to what went on between Jennifer and Himat. The first thing was the return of Jennifer's documents.

'We now have photocopies of all these,' said Himat as he returned Jennifer's paperwork. 'Now there are two accounts and the safe deposit box to sign for.' He slid one paper across the table to Jennifer saying as he did so, 'Current account in the sum of seven hundred and two dollars.' He pointed to the bottom of the paper. 'Sign here please.' Jennifer signed and Himat slid a second sheet in front of her. 'Deposit account in the sum of twelve thousand and sixty-three dollars and twelve cents. That includes the accrued interest.'

'How much?' Jennifer exclaimed.

Himat leant across the table and pointed at the figure. 'Twelve thousand . . . '

'No, no, it's okay,' said Jennifer quickly. 'I was forgetting, it sounds a lot but that'll be in Fijian dollars won't it?'

'U.S. Dollars,' said Himat. 'Your Grandfather always insisted on U.S. Dollar accounts.'

Jennifer signed without further comment. Himat passed over a cheque book, a book of deposit slips and bank statements for both accounts.

'Would you like me to set up an Internet account for you?' He asked.

'Could we leave it until later?'

'Of course, Miss Beddows, that just leaves one more signature, for the key.'

I don't know exactly what Jennifer was expecting to find in the safe deposit box but I doubt if it was paperwork. There were old diaries, out of date passports, school notebooks, sketchbooks, two small photograph albums, several loose photographs and a badly stained and crumpled chart. It appeared to be the old man's past in pictures and print. I was all for removing it and going through it back at the hotel but Jennifer demurred. She wanted it left until later although I did see her tuck one of the photographs into her handbag.

The driver that collected us from the hotel was called Raj. The car was a Volvo and as he opened the rear door for

Jennifer he said, 'Call me Raj.' He chattered continuously throughout the fifteen-minute journey mainly about his pride and joy — his car. It was air-conditioned but every time we stopped at a junction or at traffic lights he would switch it off until the car was underway again.

'I had air-conditioning fitted,' he explained. 'Unfortunately the mechanic got something wrong and he doesn't know how to fix it. I can't start the car when the air-conditioning is on.' He muttered something more under his breath that sounded to me something like, 'Bluidy mechanics.' I could understand his frustration because the car felt as if it was suffering. It would accelerate smoothly away from a junction until he switched on the aircon. At that point the car reacted as if someone had punched it in the stomach. It slowed, stuttered, then reluctantly regained speed — it was in need of some tender loving care from a mechanic who understood air-conditioning and cars.

It turned out that Raj was a hire car

driver. Mr Patel had engaged him to collect us from the hotel because his own car was late back from a routine service. I remember wondering if Mr Patel's car was in the hands of Raj's mechanic.

11

I don't know what Jennifer was expecting of our dinner date with Mr Patel but whatever it was it cannot have been what we experienced. The meal itself lasted well over three hours. It was a buffet meal with a bewildering array of foods. I counted seven different curries, three local fish dishes — my favourite being crab cooked in coconut milk — and even roast beef and Yorkshire puddings. Interspaced amongst these dishes were several bowls of chillies that the Indian members of the gathering seemed to treat as occasional snacks, popping them into their mouths and chewing away quite happily. I took one cautious nibble from one of them and it felt as if my mouth was on fire.

It was impossible for either of us to keep track of all the people we were introduced to that night. The house seemed to have a floating population, people coming and going throughout the evening with young children running around the garden whilst their parents sat around chatting and eating. I do remember talking to Himat and his brother Rajesh and learning from them that the evening gathering was a monthly affair for the Patel family and their friends. Our arrival in Fiji just happened to coincide with it.

The drinks provided were largely non-alcoholic, iced tea, fruit drinks and colas but there was a light beer which I particularly enjoyed especially after my encounter with the chillies. After the main courses were cleared away the tables were laden once again but this time with fruit, cakes and various local sweetmeats. I must confess that I made a pig of myself by eating two helpings of fried banana with ice cream and honey. It was superb.

We did eventually have the opportunity to sit and chat quietly with Mr Patel, we even used first names, his was Banerjee. In answer to Jennifer's question about how he and her grandfather had first met he explained that it was through his uncle.

'My uncle Ravi used to trade with the salvage company that your grandfather, Albert, was part of.'

'What did they trade?'

'Anything and everything, remember this was just after the war and virtually everything was in short supply. My uncle bought tools, clothing, tinned food and even on one memorable occasion two hundred bottles of saki.'

'Saki?'

'Yes, the Japanese rice wine.'

'Where on earth did they get saki?'

'From abandoned Japanese stores.'

'Well how did you meet him?'

'When Uncle bought the jeep.'

'A jeep, from my Grandfather?'

'Yes, they had several to sell, some of them brand new. Uncle bought a secondhand one. It only had two bullet holes in it. Part of the deal was for Albert to teach me to drive.'

'Did he, teach you I mean?'

'Yes I had four lessons before they had to sail again. He didn't have time to teach me how to reverse; I had to learn that myself.'

'Where did they get all this trade material?' I asked.

'Almost anywhere in this region that had been touched by the war — the Solomon Islands, Papua New Guinea, the islands that are now part of Indonesia.'

'Did they buy it?'

'I don't think so. I believe they just collected whatever had been left lying about by the various forces.'

'Was it legal?'

'When they started in business late in 1945 there weren't any rules but later of course there were. That was when they had to shut down.'

'When was that?'

'In nineteen-forty-nine, by that time they'd made a fortune.'

'From Fiji?'

'No, no, they traded all over the South Pacific. I remember Albert telling me how they sold a lot of vehicles to Australian farmers.'

'Jeeps?'

'Jeeps, trucks, even a couple of bulldozers.'

'Where on earth did they find bulldozers?'

'I don't know but I do know that near one island they found a large landing craft stranded on a reef with its cargo of vehicles intact.'

'Was there ever any mention of precious stones?' Jennifer asked.

'Not as salvage but your Grandfather did buy some here in Fiji. I told you that my Uncle bought a jeep, well after that we traded regularly. I know Albert bought a number of diamonds, eight or nine I think.'

'When was this?'

'I'm almost certain it was in nineteen-forty-nine.'

Jennifer sat back with a sigh. 'Well we know where those diamonds went and now we know where they came from.'

Mr Patel looked around as if checking if any of the few remaining guests were in hearing range. When he saw that there was nobody close by he leant towards Jennifer and spoke in a quiet voice.

'My cousin bought gold from your Grandfather years later. Daz is a dentist, he bought it for teeth.' He spread his lips and displayed his own gold fillings.

'Was he here tonight?' I asked.

'Oh no, he lives in Canada now. He left Fiji after the first military coup in the nineteen-eighties.'

At that point Himat appeared with the news that Mr Patel's car was still in the hands of the mechanic and would not be available until the following day. Despite my offering to call for a taxi Himat insisted on driving us to the hotel. Back at the Travelodge I helped Jennifer from the car then turned to thank Himat. He gripped my arm and said in a quiet voice, 'My father doesn't know about all of Albert's deals. If you need to know more contact me before you leave.'

The following morning we found the boat to take us to the Kingston Islands. I'd made an appointment by telephone the previous day with the boat's owner and skipper, Joe Singa. His son, Seru, collected us from the hotel in an elderly but immaculate Morris Oxford. Once again a short drive took us to the Bay of Islands. The boat was anchored offshore but Joe was waiting for us with a dinghy alongside a small jetty. He greeted us with cries of 'Bula', a warm handshake and a broad grin, things that were a definite improvement on our previous visit to the Bay. Both he and his son were typical Fijian males, tall, muscular men with a cheerful disposition.

Their yacht, *Yasawa Queen*, had that solid dependable look that I used to associate with MFVs when I was in the Navy. She was certainly longer and leaner than an MFV but she still looked capable of dealing with the open ocean. I liked the look of her even before I set foot on deck and I liked her even more when I'd had a look around. It was easy to see that the two men were proud of their vessel and were careful with her upkeep. Everywhere I looked I saw competence and cleanliness. Sails were neatly stowed, the engine and its compartment gleamed, the galley and the accommodation were spick and span and I finished the tour of the vessel with a good feeling about her and her crew. Jennifer agreed with me and wanted to charter the boat immediately but I urged caution. I first needed to know whether they'd ever sailed beyond Fijian waters. When I asked about this point Joe produced the logbook and showed me details of some of their longer voyages.

'Six months ago we went to the Solomon Islands,' he said turning back the pages of the logbook and pointing to the relevant entries. 'We have been as far north as Lae in Papua New Guinea and as far south as New Zealand.' Again he illustrated the point by showing us the logged entries. 'Our main work is here in the Fijian Islands but as you see we are willing to go anywhere within reason.'

I took Albert's map of the Kingston Islands from my pocket and spread it out on the chart table. 'Are you willing to take us here?' I asked.

Joe studied the map for a couple of minutes without replying then produced a large scale chart of the South Pacific and compared Albert's plotted position of the islands with the chart.

'I've heard of this place,' he said. 'It's

known as a safe anchorage. I'll take you there.' He produced a pair of dividers and did some quick measurements on the chart followed by a couple of calculations. 'Assuming good weather, six possibly seven days to get there. How long do you want to be ashore?'

'We don't know, it all depends on what we find when we get there. Allow a week although it will probably be less than that.' I replied.

'Okay, a three week charter initially.' He took a printed leaflet from a drawer and passed it to me. 'Those are my daily rates, seventy-five percent payable before departure and the balance on the day of return. Would you like to talk it over in private?'

I looked across at Jennifer and received a brief nod in reply. 'Yes,' I replied.

He immediately got to his feet. 'Take your time,' he said. 'I'll be on deck when you're ready.'

Once we were alone Jennifer said, 'I'd like your opinion. Do you think the boat is safe and are those rates reasonable?'

'The boat looks in fine condition, I

doubt if we'll find one in better shape. As for the charter rates I'm no expert but there are two men's wages to consider plus the upkeep of a boat like this with food and fuel costs on top so I do think these rates are reasonable.'

She smiled. 'I thought you liked this boat,' she said. 'How soon can we leave?'

I got to my feet. 'Come on, we'll go and ask?'

A few minutes later Joe was using his fingers to tick off various items. 'Fuel we can top up today, water also but as for food we can only order it today for delivery on Monday.'

'I need to go to the bank before we sail,' said Jennifer.

Joe glanced at his watch. 'You won't get there today, they'll be closing in about half an hour and they don't open on Saturday afternoons.'

'Can we get away just after lunch on Monday then?' I asked.

'That'll be okay with me,' replied Joe with a smile.

Jennifer nodded. 'And me,' she said.

Suddenly Joe snapped his fingers. 'I

nearly forgot to ask about communications,' he exclaimed. 'We're fitted with VHF and HF radio but if you want to make telephone calls I usually hire a satellite telephone. Do you want me to do that?'

'How long will that take to fit?' I asked.

'Oh, only a few minutes, we're fitted for but not with.'

'Cost?'

'It's included in the daily rate.'

'Okay then, let's have it fitted.'

'What do you mean,' asked Jennifer. 'Fitted for but not with?'

'It means that the wiring is permanently fitted but the actual units are only brought aboard when they are required.' I explained.

'That's correct,' said Joe. 'The reason we don't have it permanently fitted is because some clients specify that they want to be out of touch for the duration of the charter. They don't want the office calling them every time there's a problem.'

'But you've got radios, surely they can contact you on them,' said Jennifer.

'We have to carry the radios to comply with safety regulations but we don't have to accept telephone calls if the client doesn't want them and we can always arrange to be conveniently 'out of range' if necessary.'

After agreeing to arrange our own transport to the jetty on the Monday afternoon Joe rowed us ashore. Seru took us back to the hotel and as he drove away gave a cheerful cry of 'see you Monday'.

12

I spent that Saturday afternoon relaxing by the pool. Jennifer was wandering round the hotel grounds armed with a digital camera and a sketchbook. I watched her admiring and photographing a particular orchid. It took her almost twenty minutes to get the effect she wanted and I must admit I was impressed when she showed me the result. It was a work of art. If I'd photographed the same plant it would have looked okay but I could never have achieved the stunning effect that she had. It was she informed me a Tulip Cattleya orchid. About an hour later she produced another equally magnificent photograph of a Vanda orchid. She was using a small booklet purchased from the hotel shop to identify the various flowers.

Eventually she came and sat by my side. I ordered drinks and a young waitress brought them to our table.

Jennifer watched her walk away before commenting on her beauty.

'Pretty,' I replied. 'But I wouldn't have said beautiful.'

'Not the waitress, Kesa.'

'Kesa, who's Kesa?'

'Seru's wife.'

'When did you meet her?'

She laughed, opened her handbag and handed me the leaflet about the *Yasawa Queen*. 'Turn it over,' she said.

There was a photograph of the yacht with three people standing in front of it. Beneath them were a few words of introduction, they said:- 'Joe Singa, your Captain, Seru, second in command and your hostess, Seru's wife Kesa.'

'Well, well, well. I did wonder who was going to do the cooking and yes, she is extemely good-looking.'

She then produced another photograph from her handbag. I recognised it immediately as the black and white one that she'd taken from the safe deposit box. I studied it for a few minutes before commenting.

'It must be your Grandmother,' I said.

'You're like identical twins, both equally beautiful.'

She was blushing when I handed the photograph back. For a few moments she sat studying the picture before speaking. I could see tears in the corner of her eyes when she eventually spoke. 'I wasn't fishing for compliments.'

'I know,' I replied. 'I was merely telling the truth.'

'Dinner,' she said scrambling to her feet. 'I'll see you at dinner.'

Her drink sat untouched across the table from me.

The first thing I did when we met for dinner was to apologise for upsetting her earlier. Actually I didn't know how I'd upset her but I apologised just to be on the safe side. Nevertheless we ate the meal in a strained atmosphere. It wasn't until we settled at an outside table and ordered coffee that things began to improve. It was my opening remark that finally broke, the ice.

'There's still time to call this trip off Jennifer if you're having second thoughts.'

'No I don't want to do that,' she replied.

'I've been thinking about all those notebooks and diaries in the bank, the answers about Albert's past are probably all there. If we read through them first we may not need to make the trip.'

She looked up and smiled at me for the first time that evening. 'Why do you think I insisted in leaving them there,' she said. 'I want to make this trip we can go through the diaries during it.'

'I thought you might be getting homesick.'

'Oh no, but I was feeling sorry for myself this afternoon.'

'Why?'

'There were several reasons. For instance I was thinking about how my family seems to have a thing about dying young. Grandmother was younger than me when she was killed, my parents died before their time and probably this other lady, Valerie, as well.'

'Albert was in his eighties,' I retorted.

'That's true,' she said getting to her

138

feet. 'Come on walk with me through the gardens.'

It was a beautiful night. The moon's reflection lay like a silvery pathway across the waters of the harbour, the scent of frangipani perfumed the air and even the cicadas sounded happy. Jennifer took my hand.

'Before I met you,' she said. 'I had a home, a job of sorts and lots of bills I was struggling to pay. Now, because of you, that's all changed. Three months ago I was wondering whether I could afford to stay overnight in London when I visited my agent. Now I'm chartering a yacht and not worrying about the money. It's like a fairy tale.'

'Actually, it's Albert you should be thanking not me,' I replied.

We walked on in silence for several minutes before she suddenly stopped and turned to face me. She said nothing at first then suddenly rose on tiptoe and kissed me. 'Thank you for coming into my life,' she said. Without waiting to see my reaction she began to walk again with me trailing along behind her wondering what had hit me. I'd just about got my head sorted out when she stopped and turned to face me again.

'I've decided not to do that again until you start calling me Jenny.'

That time I was more prepared for her. I could see a mischievous gleam in her eyes so I decided to take up the challenge. I got no further than the first word.

'Jenny,' I said. She was in my arms in an instant.

Fijians are a religious people and the majority of them attend church on Sunday. During our wandering around Suva the following day we identified a number of different denominations but the majority of the people were headed for the Roman Catholic cathedral on Pratt Street. We joined them and sat together at the rear of the congregation throughout the morning service. I'm not a particularly religious person but for some reason I found that service a moving experience. Of course my feelings may have been unsettled by the events of the previous night or it could have been the thought of the following days at sea but whatever it was I found it emotionally disturbing.

Afterwards we strolled side by side along Victoria Parade. There were two young girls with their parents ahead of us and Jennifer remarked on how smart they looked. The girls wore white dresses with matching white lace gloves. In their hands they each carried a small Bible. Their mother wore a long, high-necked cotton dress whilst their father was attired in a simple white shirt and grey sulu. All four wore sandals without socks. Looking around I could see several other family groups all similarly attired.

'It's almost as if we've stepped back in time,' I said.

'In what way?' Jennifer asked.

'I've got photographs at home of my parents dressed in their Sunday best on their way back from church. This is almost the same.'

'I'll bet your father didn't wear a kilt like that,' said Jennifer.

'It's not a kilt. It's called a sulu here in Fiji, a lap-lap in Papua New Guinea and a sarong in Malaysia.'

'My, you are a fund of knowledge this morning. What is it called in Tonga?'

'Okay, you've got me, I haven't a clue.'

'Do they even wear them in Tonga?'

'I should imagine so, they're common throughout this region.'

'Have you ever worn one?'

'Yes, I've got one with me. Mine is just a simple length of cloth that you wrap around your waist. These here in Fiji are tailored with proper waist fastenings.'

'Doesn't yours have a proper fastening?'

'No I just tuck the loose end in at the waist.'

'What do you wear underneath?'

'Nothing — I never wear it outside of my room.'

'That sounds interesting,' she murmured.

I glanced across at her and spotted the mischievous grin that I'd seen the night before.

'Behave yourself, Jennifer you'll be giving me ideas I shouldn't have.'

'Why not?' she retorted, her grin wider than ever.

'Simply because my wise old Uncle George told me never to mix business with pleasure,' I responded.

'In that case I'll have to fire you.'

I didn't get the chance to respond because at that moment a car drew up alongside us and Seru called a cheerful 'good morning'. He'd just come from the hotel where he'd left a note for us about the arrangements for the following day. The stores were being delivered at eight a.m. and as soon as they were aboard he intended to drive round to the hotel to collect our luggage. After that we could set sail as soon as Jennifer and I had finished our business at the bank.

Later that afternoon I made use of the business facilities at the hotel to send e-mails to Charlie and Lieutenant Commander Footweller. Charlie's message was quite detailed covering what we'd discovered at the bank as well as our arrangements for the visit to the Kingston Islands. The e-mail to Jimmy Footweller merely stated our etd Fiji and our eta at the islands. Jennifer took over the computer after I'd finished, she wanted to send a message to her agent in London. I think she would also have liked to send one to her aunt in Bridlington but she opted for a postcard instead. When I asked her why she'd chosen the postcard she said that she felt it was more personal and it would give her aunt more pleasure than an e-mail.

That night while I was packing I tried to analyse my feelings for Jennifer. I knew I was growing fonder of her as each day passed but was it love? I didn't know. She was eight or nine years younger than me and was extremely good-looking, with a fine figure and a great sense of humour. For the last few days she'd given me the impression that she wanted me to take things further than the few kisses we'd exchanged but would I be taking advantage of her if I did? Was she merely flirting or was she serious? Were the tropical conditions and our close proximity to each other to blame? In the end I decided that speculation was a waste of time and energy — I could only wait and see how things would develop. I slept badly once again.

13

There were virtually none of the formalities that I associated with a ship leaving harbour the following morning. There was an immigration officer on board the yacht and he briefly glanced at our passports. Having satisfied himself that we were who we purported to be he wished us bon voyage before Seru rowed him ashore. Once Seru returned and the dinghy was lifted inboard we were free to leave. As the anchor was weighed and the engine started I felt a sense of excitement, eager anticipation at what was to come.

Whilst Joe and Seru were busy with the leaving harbour routine Kesa introduced herself to us. Taking us below she showed us the cabins that she'd allocated. Both were double cabins.

'We normally carry eight passengers so there's plenty of room,' she explained. 'I had to check with the hotel to see if you were in one room or two. Men never think of things like that.'

After showing us the bathroom and toilet arrangements she left us to stow our gear. That took me about ten minutes. I then changed into a pair of shorts and a sleeveless shirt and set out to explore our new temporary home.

Outside my cabin was a narrow passageway running fore and aft, a passage that separated Jennifer's cabin from mine. I made my way forward into the bows where I found as I expected a sail locker in the forepeak. Then, moving aft, came two empty cabins, double berths but because of the shape of the hull were smaller than ours. Between those cabins and ours were the two small bathrooms, one either side of the passage. Each consisted of a shower, washbasin and toilet. Beyond our cabins lay the main cabin with seating arrangements for about ten people and behind a small partition on the starboard side lay the galley. Opposite the galley on the port side was a chart table with a range of instrumentation above it. A companion-way led up from there to the cockpit

146

beyond which lay the engine compartment and accommodation for four crew members.

On deck above the crews' accommodation were stowed the dinghy and an inflatable fitted with an outboard engine. A single davit was positioned aft in order to lower them over the side when necessary. On the main cabin top were two white canisters each holding a ten-man liferaft and between them was an emergency position-indicating radio beacon. It was comforting to know that the vessel was well supplied with emergency equipment but I sincerely hoped that we'd never have to use it.

Joe was at the helm and I stood alongside him getting the feel of the boat as we moved out of the sheltered waters of the harbour. We were running under power and as I watched Joe operate what appeared to be a gear lever, the engine note changed from a gentle murmur to a deep-throated growl.

'Is that a different engine?' I asked.

He nodded. 'Yes,' he said. 'It's an engine arrangement I've never come across before, two engines operating in tandem on the same shaft but with only one engine driving at a time.'

I pointed to the gear lever. 'Does that switch one engine on and the other off then?'

'No not quite, both engines are running but that lever switches the drive from one to the other.' He pressed a button alongside the lever. 'That's the harbour engine switched off we're now running on the main.'

'I was expecting us to be under sail once we cleared the harbour,' I said.

'There's too much traffic at present.' He pointed ahead. 'Fishing boats, yachts and ferries, once we're clear of that lot we'll get the sails up.'

I looked back at the land. 'Are we heading south?' I asked.

'For a short while, I want to pass south of Viti Levu then turn north when we're clear of the Mamanuca Islands.'

'When do you expect to turn?'

'Sometime in the early hours of the morning.'

'Who'll be on watch then?'

'Me — Seru and I work six and six

about. I've got the helm now until six this evening then Seru takes over until midnight. We find the routine works well. If either of us needs a break then Kesa can take over for a while.'

'I'm willing to stand a watch,' I said.

He glanced across at me in surprise. 'You've sailed before?'

'Yes, but not for some time, I'd like to get my hand in again.'

He stepped aside and motioned me behind the wheel. 'There's no time like the present,' he said with a grin.

The yacht had a traditional wooden wheel with brass enhancements and the polished timber spokes fitted smoothly into my palms. It felt great to be handling a vessel once more. Joe stood beside me and occasionally glanced astern at the wake. I know there were a few kinks in the wake initially but once I'd got the feel of her it ran arrow straight. I looked back myself to check. It was then that I noticed Jennifer standing behind us. She gave me a mock salute and motioned to me to carry on. However, we were approaching a line of fishing boats and Joe wasn't willing to risk my ship handling so early in the voyage. He took the wheel again.

I moved back to stand beside Jennifer to allow Joe to concentrate on weaving through the line of boats. I remember turning to Jennifer and asking if she was okay.

'Actually I'm not too good,' she replied. 'I'm feeling a bit of a wimp, we've barely started and I'm already rather queasy.'

'So am I,' I said. 'There's nothing wimpish about feeling a bit uneasy when you first put to sea. I always try to stay in the fresh air until I've got my sea legs.'

'But you were a sailor.'

'So was Lord Nelson and he was seasick every time he went to sea. After the first day or so he was okay. I'm the same.'

We sat for a while at the rear of the cockpit with me pointing out various places of interest on the shore in an attempt to keep her mind off seasickness. It didn't work for long though. She suddenly gave a groan and made a dash for the heads. I followed her down below but Kesa saw what was happening and forestalled me.

'Don't worry,' she said. 'I'll look after her. There's always someone feeling unwell when we first set off.'

Back on deck Joe soon had me behind the wheel again. It was while he was standing beside me that I asked where the yacht was built.

'America,' he replied. 'She was built for a millionaire businessman. He'd had a heart attack and his doctor told him that he had to relax more so he had this built for his relaxation.'

'Sorry, I thought she was yours.'

'She is now or rather she will be if we ever get the mortgage paid off.'

'What happened to the millionaire?'

'Six years ago a run crew brought the yacht across from the States. I was employed to skipper her here but we hardly ever went to sea.'

'Why not?'

'He couldn't let his business go. The first time he and his wife came out they were supposed be having a two-week cruise but we spent two days at sea and the rest in Suva harbour so he could get ashore to send faxes to the office. That was when we fitted the satellite communications.'

'What happened then?'

'He tried twice more, the first time he managed four days and then six months later he only managed one night aboard. That was the last I saw of him.'

'Did he put her up for sale then?'

'Not then, about six months later. By that time I was bored stiff, the yacht had grown weed and barnacles and the crew apart from me had been paid off.'

'How did you come to buy her?'

'I actually tried to lease her but they came back with an offer to sell. We've been running her as a family concern ever since.'

'She's a fine boat,' I said.

He nodded agreement. 'I'm looking forward to letting her run. It's not often we get the chance of a long passage. Normally we're just pottering about in the islands with only a few hours at sea between stops.'

'Who charters her normally?'

'Mainly companies, they send their

executives for what they call bonding sessions.'

'Do they, bond I mean?'

'It depends who they bring with them.'

I glanced across at him and he noticed my questioning look.

'Sometimes the wives they bring are only wives for a fortnight.'

'Ah, I see your point. Do they ever cause trouble?'

'Very rarely, I did put one party ashore after four days of constant trouble but the company concerned paid for the full trip so I had no complaints. People are people, sometimes they bond at other times they bicker.'

A small cargo vessel was approaching on a course that would pass close across our bows. Joe demonstrated his growing confidence in my abilities by allowing me to alter course around her stern, once we were clear of her Joe asked the purpose of our trip. I explained about Albert and how Jennifer wanted to trace her grandfather's past. When I mentioned the grave of Valerie Beddows he looked concerned.

'Sometimes,' he said. 'The past is best left undisturbed.'

Shortly afterwards he further demonstrated his confidence in my abilities by going below. He returned a few minutes later with Seru and working as a team they soon had a mainsail hoisted. Joe took over the wheel then and for about fifteen minutes allowed the yacht to run under sail and power. Once he was satisfied he shut down the engine and we proceeded under sail alone. The motion was easier and without the background throb of the engine the whole atmosphere changed. The smack of waves against the hull and the hiss of spray over the bow interspersed with the occasional slap of rigging against the mast was almost music to my ears. I hadn't realised how much I'd missed the sounds of the sea until that moment.

Kesa interrupted my reverie by coming up on deck with news of Jennifer. Apparently she was lying down and had no intention of joining me for dinner. Kesa had given her a couple of travel pills and she was already asleep. There appeared to be little likelihood of my seeing her again until the following day. However, she had asked Kesa to give me the parcel of notebooks that we'd collected from the bank that morning.

I turned in early that evening and lying in my bunk I examined the notebooks. They appeared to be in date order with the earliest being a small leather-bound diary dated 1941. It was clear that at some time it had been immersed in water because a number of the pencilled entries were so badly stained that they were unreadable. Those entries that I could read were familiar from my days in the Navy, FWE — finished with engines, FA — full away and so on. There were single letter notations alongside these entries that I assumed indicated the port of arrival or departure. On the day that his wife was killed, 9th May 1941, he'd written in capital letters in the diary the words 'Homeward Bound'. Little did he know what would greet him when he got there.

14

19th July 1941

Albert Beddows dropped his kitbag and looked around in desperation trying to visualise where his home had once stood. There should have been a row of terraced houses but instead he was confronted by heaps of rubble. At least five houses had been completely demolished whilst further down the terrace the skeletal remains of other houses still stood without roofs, windows or doors. A staircase, supported by the remnants of an interior wall, led upwards but there was nothing above it; a staircase to nowhere. A chimney-stack stood in solitary isolation the black metal fireplaces at ground and first floor level still firmly in place.

An old man picked his way carefully along the terrace leaning heavily on a stick. Albert didn't recognise him at first.

'Is that you Albert, Albert Beddows?'

The old man's voice wavered uncertainly.

'Yes, what the hell happened here?'

'I'm Billy Webster. Do you remember we lived at number twelve?' He waved his stick towards one of the roofless houses.

'I didn't recognise you. Where's everybody gone?' Albert pointed to the ruined homes.

'You don't know? Oh Christ Albert I'm sorry. Hasn't anybody told you?'

'What happened, Mr Webster, where're my wife and family?' Albert's frantic request was almost shouted at the old man.

'They're dead son, your wife and your parents. The baby's alive though.'

'Baby?'

'Your son, he was born just weeks before the bombs came. He was in his pram under the staircase.' Using his stick he pointed at the isolated staircase.

'When did it happen, when did the bombers come?'

'Two months ago, May 9th.'

'Why weren't they in the shelter?'

The old man lifted his stick again and pointed at a larger heap of rubble at the far end of the terrace. 'Jerry hit that the night before. We took seventeen dead out of there.'

Albert's legs suddenly couldn't support him any longer. He sat abruptly amongst the brick dust, his head hanging between his knees. The old man looked around uncertainly as if not knowing what to do about the young man at his feet. Then as if suddenly remembering he spoke again. 'Your brother was here,' he said.

At first there was no reaction from Albert and then he slowly lifted his head and spoke. 'Brian was here?'

'Yes, the next day. They took the baby.'

'They?'

'Him and his wife.'

Albert nodded then pulled his kitbag towards him and opened the top. From it he lifted an object wrapped in a towel and removing the towel revealed a bottle of rum. He broke the seal and took a long swallow of the fiery liquid. Holding the bottle up to the old man he simply said, 'Join me?'

Dropping his stick he took the bottle in both hands and shakily held it to his lips and took one deep draught. Wiping the neck of the bottle on his coat sleeve he reluctantly handed it back. Albert rammed the cork back into the bottle and got to his feet. He looked around again at the scene of devastation that had once been a neat terrace of homes. As he did so the old man began to mumble quietly as if to himself.

'They've all gone, the Johnsons, Betty White, Tom Porter, young Billy Pearson, him that was wounded in Norway . . . '

Albert walked away, his kitbag on his shoulder and the rum bottle in his other hand. The old man didn't notice at first but when he did he looked down at the ground in front of him and shouted. 'My stick Albert, I need my bloody stick.' Albert walked on completely oblivious to his predicament.

Almost two hours later Albert found himself in Paragon railway station. He had no idea how he had got there. His stomach was telling him that he needed food, his feet were sore and his head ached. In the station buffet he was able to buy a sausage roll of dubious quality, a cheese sandwich and a mug of tea. He mechanically worked his way through the scratch meal while his mind considered what options were open to him. He'd paid off his ship early that morning in Liverpool and he'd no desire to go back there, his home in Hull was gone and that left him with two possibilities. He could stay overnight in the seaman's mission or he could make his way to his brother's home in Driffield. Half an hour later he boarded the train to Driffield.

Brian Beddows, Albert's brother, was, like Albert, an engineer. However, whilst Albert was a marine engineer Brian worked with aircraft. He was based at Driffield aerodrome. His wife Brenda worked as an assistant in her father's grocery shop. Her parents lived above the shop whilst she and Brian rented a tiny old-fashioned cottage close by. The cottage had a kitchen and a living room downstairs and two bedrooms above. Their water supply came from one tap in the yard outside. The toilet was also outside in the yard as it was in adjacent cottages. The one advantage they had

160

over their immediate neighbours was that they were not dependent on a portable galvanised tub for bathing, they were able to utilise the facilities of a proper bathroom in her parents' home. That evening Brian was on his way back to the cottage having just had a bath when he spotted Albert walking tiredly up the street.

The two brothers met and shook hands without speaking. Brian looked at Albert's drawn features and could see the pain of loss reflected in his brother's eyes.

'Did you get my letter?' He asked.

'No. I didn't know until today.'

'Oh Christ Bert, I'm sorry. The company said they'd let you know as well.'

'I never knew a thing until I went home today. Home,' he said bitterly, 'half a wall and a staircase, no wife and no parents.'

'They didn't suffer Bert, they were outside and the blast killed them instantly. There was hardly a mark on them.'

'How did the baby survive?'

'He was under that staircase in his

pram. When the warden found him he was covered in dust, crying but otherwise unhurt. He would have died in the fire if he hadn't been crying.'

'How did you find out?'

'The warden was Tommy Brewer, he rang the aerodrome. Our station commander let me take a truck so I picked up Brenda and went straight down there.'

'What was it like?'

'Terrible, they were still digging bodies out. Elizabeth, Mum and Dad were laid under blankets in the street. I had to identify them and about a dozen others, people we grew up with.'

Brian suddenly reached across and gripped his brother's arm. 'Come on,' he said. 'Let's get you inside you look dead beat.'

Half an hour later having devoured a plate of rabbit stew Albert was asleep in an armchair by the dying embers of the fire. Beside him on the hearth sat a half-finished mug of tea. Brian and Brenda were talking quietly in the kitchen.

'I've made up the camp bed for him in

the spare room,' said Brenda.

'Just for tonight I think we'll leave him where he is,' Brian replied.

'Is he planning to stay with us throughout his leave?'

'I don't know love. I've hardly had chance to speak to him.'

'Does he know about the baby?'

'I think so. He talked to old Billy Webster.'

'You will tell him that I'd like to keep the child,' pleaded Brenda.

'Of course love but I'll leave it for a couple of days. He hasn't had chance to come to terms with Elizabeth's death yet.'

Brian got to his feet, cautiously opened the door to the living room and peered in at his brother. Albert never stirred. Turning back to his wife he motioned towards the stairs. 'We'd better get some sleep ourselves before the baby wakes.'

Two days later Albert borrowed a bicycle and rode back into Hull to visit the graves of both his wife and his parents. He sat beside Elizabeth's grave for two hours and talked almost continuously. Anyone passing close by must have

163

thought he was mentally disturbed and in a way he probably was. He was still suffering from the shock of discovering that he no longer had a wife and a home but he'd recovered sufficiently enough to think about his son's future. He talked of the possibilty of leaving the child in Brenda's care and how he himself could provide financial support. On the subject of christening the child he mentioned several names, names that they had discussed when Elizabeth first realised she was pregnant but hadn't finally decided upon before she was killed. Two hours later he left the cemetery convinced in his own mind that Elizabeth had helped him come to a decision. The child would be christened David and would remain in the care of Brian and Brenda.

Still riding the borrowed bicycle he made his way into the centre of Hull and paid a visit to the shipping office in Posterngate where he amended the details of his next of kin. His next stop was at the registry office to record his son's birth, something he and Elizabeth had planned to do together once they had decided on a name. Much later he rode wearily back into Driffield. The child was christened the following Sunday and the next day Albert went back to his ship secure in the knowledge that he'd done the best he could for his son.

15

I spent fifteen minutes sorting through the various diaries and notebooks before putting them aside and switching off the bunk light. I lay awake for a while going over in my mind what I'd read. As far as I could see the diaries had been damaged by immersion in water but much of what they contained had been written up and recorded later in the notebooks. The neatly handwritten notebooks appeared to contain a more detailed list of events in Albert's life. It was if the man who was so secretive in life wanted to explain why after his death. Was the information in the notebooks intended for his son David, the son he'd supported financially but barely knew? I fell asleep pondering that thought.

Knowing that the early morning alteration of course would probably involve sail changes I had planned to help if I could. However, I finally awoke at

0700, three hours after the course alteration. On deck I found Seru at the helm and the yacht sliding smoothly along under a single headsail and a reefed main. I breakfasted alone but shortly afterwards I was pleased to see Jennifer on her feet and obviously feeling hungry. She joined me on deck still munching on a slice of toast, her brief bout of seasickness a thing of the past.

'Feeling better?' I asked.

She nodded a reply, swallowed the last of the toast then waved her hand towards the line of islands on our starboard side.

'Isn't that a wonderful sight,' she cried.

'My mother said that once in just the same way. We were sailing off Malta and she waved towards the islands just as you did then.'

'That's the first time you've mentioned her, is she still alive?'

'Very much so, in fact both my parents are although they are divorced. Mother's now married to a sheep farmer in New Zealand and Dad lives in Florida.'

'Is he married?'

'To be honest, I don't know. I hardly

167

ever hear from him. Mother still sends a card and a note at Christmas and she still remembers my birthday but as for Dad he's been virtually out of contact since the divorce.'

'What happened, why did they split up?'

'I asked Mother that same question and all she said was, 'we grew up and grew apart.' Personally I think something happened when Dad was posted to the States.'

'Posted?'

'Oh yes, didn't I say, he was in the Navy. He was posted to a naval base near Jacksonville as a liaison officer and I'm sure something happened while he was there that caused the breakup.'

'Where were you when it happened?'

'Portsmouth, I was a young midshipman on my first ship. Mother came down one weekend and told me about it. By then the pair of them had sold our home, split the proceeds and were ready to head off in different directions. She said they'd waited until I was settled in the Navy before parting.'

'Is that when Uncle George came into the picture?'

'Yes, you could say that. He was the black sheep of Dad's family but he agreed to give me somewhere to stay when I was on leave. I had great respect for George.'

'What did he do for a living?'

'He was a turf accountant, a racecourse bookie, a very shrewd man who channelled his winnings into all kinds of successful ventures.'

'Then why was he considered the black sheep of the family?'

'They're a straight-laced lot, puritanical almost. In that kind of family a bookie was one step away from a devil's disciple.'

'How did he die?'

'The death certificate said pneumonia but he was being treated for a serious liver condition at the time so that could have been the indirect cause. He told me about three weeks before he died that he hadn't long to live and that was before he contracted pneumonia.'

'Were you there when he died?'

'No, I was at sea but I did get to the funeral. Dad and I were the only family members there but there were nearly two hundred of George's friends and associates.'

'He must have been popular.'

'He was, with everyone but his family. Mind you when the will was read there were twenty-two family members present. Most of them left disappointed. I'm the new black sheep.'

'You are, why?'

'Because I broke with family tradition, just as George did.'

'How?'

'It's a long story but basically the history of Dad's side of the family is of service. The eldest son was always destined to join the Church and the second son the Army. The family hymn was 'Onward Christian Soldiers' so you can imagine what it was like when first Dad broke with tradition and joined the Navy and then George became a bookie.'

'But surely the Navy would be okay?'

'It was accepted eventually but when I inherited some of George's money and left the Navy then I became persona non grata.'

'That can't be right, not in this day and age.'

'I have two male cousins; one is a vicar and the other an army colonel whilst I am a private investigator. In a family that can boast of at least one bishop and two generals in its ancestry private investigators don't really fit.'

'This is the twenty-first century for goodness sake.'

'True, but most of the family are still living in the nineteenth. I have a great aunt who believes that jazz was invented by the devil and that television will never catch on.'

Jennifer burst into laughter. 'You're joking of course,' she spluttered.

'No, that's the truth, but then she is in her nineties.'

I recall that particular conversation continuing for some time. We talked about the peculiarities of my family and how things had changed for me since the death of my uncle. Before George's death I could remember receiving invites to attend weddings, christenings, anniversaries of various kinds and funerals even when the family knew my ship was thousands of miles away. I was a family member therefore I was included in the invitations despite the fact that they knew I couldn't attend. However, after George's death and my acceptance of his money the only contact the family had with me was to inform me of deaths. My father didn't think too kindly of the family either. At the funeral he made a comment to me about them. He called them a bunch of old farts living on past glories and he included his own father in that statement. Longevity runs in the family.

Kesa came on deck and took over the wheel for a while to give Seru a break and Jennifer went over to talk to her. I took the opportunity to go below to look at the first of Alfred's notebooks again. I could understand that in wartime letters would be delayed or lost altogether which would explain why Alfred knew nothing of his wife's death until he arrived home. However, he seemed to know nothing of the bombing that had taken place in Hull and that puzzled me. Surely he must have heard news broadcasts from the B.B.C. or other radio stations. The answer was in that first notebook — the broadcasts spoke only of a 'north-east coast town' being attacked. There was a newspaper clipping stuck on one page that mentioned a figure of almost 87,000 houses in Hull being destroyed or damaged throughout the war, that particular 'north-east coast town' must have featured regularly in the news broadcasts.

The more I read of those notes the more I began to realise that they were not in chronological order. They seemed to be more of an aide-memoire. He'd certainly transcribed notes from the diaries into the notebooks but he seemed to have added other items just when he'd remembered them. For example the newspaper clipping about the houses destroyed and damaged must have been from after the war but Albert had inserted it in his 1941 notes. There were other comments about rationing, identity cards and gas masks that seemed to have been slotted in anywhere in order to jog his memory. It was almost as if he was planning to write the whole thing up later in book form but had never got around to it.

On one page he made mention of the effect that double summer time was having on the people of Britain. He noted seeing men and women still working in gardens and allotments at ten or eleven at night in order to eke out their ration allowances. Later, on the same page, he talked about the convoy routes to Russia in the summertime with virtually twenty-four hours of daylight to endure. He and his fellow seafarers seemed to prefer the harsh winter weather conditions of Arctic waters that tended to hide them from their German attackers. These of course were the days when radar was still in its infancy and for the most part was virtually unknown at sea.

Later that day I asked Jennifer if she wanted the notebooks returning but she said no. There were she said a number of technical terms in them that she didn't understand so she wanted me to go through them first and to give her a sanitised version of their contents later. I remember wondering at the time whether that was the real reason or whether she was worried that she'd come across some dark deed in Albert's past that would cause her to reconsider her reasons for being onboard the yacht. I really believed that she was enjoying the novelty of being at sea and didn't want that enjoyment spoilt. I was secretly pleased to be able to keep the books because despite their disjointed contents I was finding them fascinating. Albert Beddows had got under my skin and the more I read the more intrigued I became.

16

When I was at school our history lessons never covered the events of the Second World War and it wasn't until I joined the Navy that I learned of the British invasion of Iceland in 1940. After Denmark was overrun by the German armed forces a decision was taken in Britain to invade Iceland to prevent it falling into German hands. The reason for this was to prevent the island being used as a base to attack our Atlantic convoys. The following year Hvalfjord in Iceland became one of the assembly points for convoys to Russia.

Albert's notes described Hvalfjord as a terrible forbidding wasteland that in winter was exposed to howling gales and fierce winter weather. So much so that convoys anchored there had to maintain full seagoing watches because of the danger of dragging anchors resulting in collisions between the heavily laden merchant ships. Vessels from Britain bound for Russia first assembled in Loch Ewe in Scotland. Although remote, Albert described Loch Ewe as being well sheltered from Atlantic storms and a safe anchorage for many ships. From there the ships proceeded in convoy to Iceland where they were joined by ships from America. This larger convoy then proceeded to Russia.

The first of these Russian convoys that Albert was part of was designated PQ1. It sailed from Iceland late in September 1941 and reached Archangel on the 11th October safely. On the second convoy, PQ8, the ships survived the voyage until they were in sight of the safety of the Kola Inlet and the port of Murmansk. In the entrance to the Kola Inlet one merchant ship and one escort were torpedoed and sunk. Although the rest of that particular convoy arrived in Murmansk safely several ships were later sunk or were badly damaged by the repeated air attacks whilst they were discharging their cargoes in port.

In his notes Albert failed to name any of the ships involved, he seemed perfectly content to designate each by a single letter. I assumed that the letter was the first letter of each ship's name but without having a list of the ships in each convoy I would never know for certain. For PQ17, the last Russian convoy that he sailed on, Albert didn't seem to know how many ships were involved. He certainly designated several by individual letters, probably those that set off from Loch Ewe, but when the larger convoy sailed from Hvalfjord he merely noted more than forty merchant ships and a considerable escort.

PQ17 left Hvalfjord on the 27th June 1942. It was one of the largest convoys ever to attempt to run the gauntlet from Iceland to Russia. At that time of year the weather was largely fair and there were virtually no hours of darkness to shelter the ships from German scout aircraft. Once these aircraft had located the convoy they would remain just out of range of the anti-aircraft guns and transmit homing signals for submarines and other attack aircraft. Despite being attacked several times the convoy was still largely intact when the order to scatter was given on the 4th July. With hindsight we now know that the order for the escorts to leave the convoy and for the merchant ships to scatter and make their way independently to Russia was a tragic error. It was given in the mistaken belief that the convoy was about to be attacked by heavy units of the German Navy. Only a handful of the merchant ships eventually reached Russian ports.

I read on for a further ten minutes before putting the notebook aside. I made my way out on deck where I was joined a short while later by Jennifer. We sat together in silence for a while, I trying to come to terms with what I had just read whilst Jennifer sat in patient silence. It was Jennifer though who eventually broke the silence.

'Is anything wrong?' She asked.

'I've just been reading Albert's experiences on PQ17. Do you remember I told you about that convoy?'

'Yes, that's when his ship was torpedoed.'

'Twice, he was torpedoed twice.'

'I don't understand how could he be torpedoed twice?'

'When the convoy scattered Albert's ship headed at full speed to the north. They were trying to reach the edge of the Arctic ice field.'

'Why?'

'The theory was that if they reached it then the floating pack ice would protect them from torpedoes.'

'I presume that they didn't make it.'

'His ship was sunk the next morning before they reached the ice.' I took hold of her hand before continuing. 'Out of sixty-four men onboard seventeen survived. They were picked up a few hours later by another merchant ship that was trying to reach the ice field.'

'Was that sunk as well?' Jennifer asked.

'Yes, Albert had barely had time to put on dry clothes when he found himself abandoning ship once again.'

'What happened then?'

'He managed to get into a lifeboat and they rowed and sailed for five days towards land before being picked up by a Russian minesweeper. The survivors were landed near Murmansk and Albert spent several days in hospital.'

'Was that when they amputated his toes?'

'Yes, the three smallest toes on his right foot. He says in his notes that if he'd been in the lifeboat another day he'd have probably lost his entire foot to frostbite.'

'How many others survived?'

'From Albert's original ship five men eventually got back to England.'

We both sat in silence for a while. Having myself sailed in Arctic waters I could visualise the icy conditions that Albert and his shipmates had to endure. It did seem strange though to be thinking of the frozen North whilst we were sitting in warm sunshine with the blue of the Pacific Ocean stretching out before us as far as the shimmering horizon. It was Jennifer who broke the silence once again.

'Do you think he lost his nerve?'

'Albert? No, not for one minute, he jumped from the frying pan into the fire as far as convoys were concerned.'

'But Brenda said he refused to go on another.'

'He refused to go on another Arctic convoy he joined a convoy heading for Malta instead.'

'Was that as bad?'

'He described the conditions as horrific but I think he had a sense of humour despite everything he went through.'

'What do you mean?'

'There's a little note that says that the attacks by sea and air were just as fierce as on the Russian convoys but if your ship was sunk at least the water was warm.'

'Was his ship sunk?'

'No, he came through that okay.'

'What did he do next?'

'I don't know, I haven't read any further yet.'

Seru intervened at that point with a request that I take over the wheel. I think he intended to take a short break but by the time he returned I was enjoying myself so much that he left me to it. In the end I had control of the helm for two hours. Jennifer sat beside me enthralled by the antics of a school of dolphins that travelled with us for some considerable time. They rode the bow wave, slid beneath the hull only to leap from the sea on the other side and crossed the bow with barely inches to spare. They were so close that Jennifer was able to reach out and touch one as it raced past. At one point she dashed below for her camera and managed to take several superb photographs, pictures that eventually helped her produce a number of book illustrations.

Later that day, in the early evening, I was standing by Joe in the cockpit. Kesa and Jennifer were sitting together by the forehatch. They appeared to be having an animated conversation punctuated at intervals by bursts of laughter.

'Those two seem to be getting on well together,' I remarked.

'Yes, it's nice to see. Sometimes it's very different,' Joe replied.

'What do you mean?'

He turned and looked at me. 'Just now and then we get a group who consider us as the hired help, menials who only get spoken to when they want something.'

'You're not serious, not in this day and age.'

He chuckled. 'Would you believe we had one woman who refused to sail with us because we were black; she said it was impossible for us to know how to navigate safely.'

'Didn't you tell her that your people had been sailing across the Pacific for hundreds of years?'

'It wouldn't have helped. She stayed in the hotel but her husband came with us. He was worse if anything, he kept addressing us as 'boy'. He never once called us by name, it was always 'hey boy do this'. Seru didn't help matters he kept touching his forehead and saying 'yes massah' in reply. The poor guy couldn't see that Seru was taking the mickey out of him.'

'What nationality was he?'

'He came aboard with an Australian party but originally he was from South Africa. I think the Aussies could see what Seru was doing but if they did they didn't enlighten him.'

'Do you often get people like that?'

'No, fortunately they are the exception we get along quite happily with most people.'

17

When the Second World War came to an abrupt end after the dropping of atomic bombs on Hiroshima and Nagasaki Albert Beddows was aboard a vessel operating in Pacific waters. Although reserved he was popular amongst his fellow officers largely because of his work. He was known as a first rate engineer who was never late on watch and was always willing to cover for any fellow officer who for any reason was unable to fulfil his duties. His senior officer, the chief engineer, once described him as being 'quietly competent' and that was probably a perfect description of Albert at that stage in his life. It came as quite a surprise to his seniors therefore when he stepped out of character and volunteered to take part in what they considered to be a hair-brained scheme.

Albert and his fellow officers were aboard a vessel that was in dire need of a major refit. For the previous eighteen months the *SS Aruba Star* had been nursed along, kept afloat by the judicious use of the welding torch, cannibalised spares and the ingenuity of her crew. They already knew that when they arrived in Sydney at the culmination of their current voyage the vessel would not sail again without undergoing a major overhaul. That meant they would probably be out of work.

Aruba Star had been used in support of the allied forces fighting the Japanese. She'd transported everything from chocolate bars to cannon shells and bicycles to bullets. In forming part of the supply train for the armed forces she herself had been subjected to bombing and shellfire. Fortunately she had survived without any direct hits but several near misses had caused substantial damage to an already battered hull. On one occasion the damage was so bad that she had to be beached in order for patches to be welded below the waterline. The island chosen for the beaching had been the subject of fierce fighting but the war had moved on across the Pacific leaving the detritus of battle behind.

Whilst Albert and his fellow engineers were busy repairing the hull other members of the ship's company were exploring the beach and its immediate surroundings. A few hundred yards along the beach from where the ship lay were two stranded landing craft, both badly damaged. In one, a tank lay on its side its useless gun pointing skywards whilst its companion was empty except for sand and a foot of seawater. A third landing craft sat high, and apparently dry, about five hundred yards offshore. It was stranded on a reef.

Two officers, Second Officer Philip Grundy, a Canadian, and Harry Walker the Third Radio Officer, a Liverpudlian, decided to investigate that third landing craft. They swam out and boarded the craft using a rope ladder that had been left conveniently dangling over the side. All that remained of the small wheelhouse was a mass of twisted metal and a series of ominously dark stains but apart from that the vessel appeared to be undamaged

187

above the waterline. The cargo deck was virtually dry and its cargo was still in situ — one bulldozer, one lorry and two jeeps.

That evening after the rising tide had lifted *Aruba Star* safely back into an upright position in the lagoon the talk in the officer's messroom centred on that third landing craft and her cargo. It was then that the initial idea for the Auspac Marine Salvage Company was born. The discussion originally centred on how to recover the stranded vehicles.

'A tug, pull the craft off the reef and beach it,' said Harry Walker.

'No you might tear the bottom out of her and lose the lot,' replied Philip Grundy.

'What do you suggest then?'

'A raft; float it out there, lower the bow doors and take them ashore one by one.'

'How would we get them onto the raft?'

'Drive them on.'

'Hang on a minute,' interjected Albert. 'Don't those vehicles belong to the army?'

'They and the vessel they are on have been abandoned so they should be the subject of normal marine salvage laws,' said a fourth voice, that of the Chief Officer, Derek Fitzpatrick.

'Do they still apply in wartime?' Albert asked.

'I think so, in fact I'm sure they do.'

'You'd never start the engines,' said Harry returning to the original argument.

'The batteries would be flat,' agreed Albert, 'but if you replaced them and checked that the ignition system was dry they probably would start.' He paused briefly before continuing. 'The fuel might have condensation in it so you'd probably have to drain that off and replace it.'

'There's more salvage out there than just those vehicles,' muttered Derek thoughtfully.

'There is?'

'Certainly, think about it, when this war's over there has to be a great deal of rebuilding. Scrap metal could be in great demand. Not iron and steel so much as the more expensive metals, phosphor-bronze, copper, brass and lead.'

'There are six phosphor-bronze propellors on those three landing craft,' said Philip.

'And brass fittings and copper pipes,' added Albert.

The chief engineer interrupted the conversation at that point by reminding them that they were due to sail at first light and suggesting that sleep might be a good idea. Although at that point the conversation ceased the idea of forming a salvage company gained momentum. Six weeks later with the war at an end and their future uncertain the idea began to take a more tangible form.

A week before *Aruba Star* arrived in Sydney a radio-telegram was received confirming that the crew was to be paid off on arrival in port. The captain and the chief engineer were to remain with the ship until a survey of the vessel had been completed but the remainder of the officers and crew were no longer required. For men like Albert Beddows this meant living in a seamen's hostel until a berth on another ship could be found. However, it was Derek Fitzpatrick who came up with an alternative suggestion for employment. He called a meeting of the officers the day after the radio-telegram arrived.

There were fourteen men in the messroom when he began to speak but gradually, as he enlarged on his idea of forming a salvage company, men got to their feet and left the room. Many had wives and families that they were eager to return to, others simply thought the idea was too hair-brained to contemplate but a handful remained in their seats. In addition to Derek those few that remained were Philip Grundy, Harry Walker and Albert Beddows.

'Well that went down like a lead balloon,' said Harry, looking round at the now empty seats.

'I haven't finished yet,' replied Derek. 'I'd like to invite Bill Toomey, the bosun, to join us, has anyone got any objection to that?'

'I've no objection,' said Philip, 'but what is he going to be bosun of?'

A grin spread over Derek's face. 'I've been saving that till last. My father has agreed to throw in his lot with us.'

'Your father . . .' muttered Harry uncertainly.

'He owns an auxiliary schooner,'

exclaimed Derek in triumph. 'He's agreed to let us use it for a trial period.'

There was a stunned silence for a few seconds then everyone started talking at once. Derek held his hands up appealing for silence. 'Okay, one at a time.'

'How long is a trial period?' asked Philip.

'Six months.'

'We'll be paying for stores and fuel I suppose,' said Harry.

'I've already spoken to the old man about that. He's willing to let us have some of the surplus stores from aboard here when we reach Sydney.'

'Assuming we can recover those vehicles we saw on that landing craft how would we dispose of them?' This time it was Albert who spoke.

'I'm hoping Dad can help us there. He's been trading along the Aussie coast throughout the war but he used to run round the islands on a regular basis,' replied Derek.

'When did you contact your father?' Philip asked.

'I sent him an airmail letter from Suva

and he replied by radio-telegram this morning.' He pulled a telegram form from his pocket and began to read. 'Agree in principle to six month trial stop Request you confirm stop will meet in Sydney stop Dad.' He looked round at the three others. 'Well,' he asked, 'do I send him a confirmation, do I tell him we're going to do it?' The three others answered yes almost simultaneously and after an exchange of handshakes the Auspac Marine Salvage Company became a reality. Half an hour later with the radio telegram safely despatched Bill Toomey, the bosun, agreed to join the Company.

Bill had been born in Wallsend-on-Tyne within sight and sound of the vast shipyards. From his bedroom window he could see the upperworks of ships and an array of dockside cranes and the sound of rivetting was with him throughout his childhood. His father and his elder brother worked in the shipyard but Bill had no wish to follow in their footsteps. Instead, as soon as he was old enough, he became a seaman. In 1945 when he agreed to join the others he was fifty years old, single, as strong as an ox and with a wealth of seagoing experience behind him.

Duncan Fitzpatrick, Derek's father, was in his late fifties. He wasn't sure of his exact age because his mother hadn't bothered to register his birth but from an early age he was sure of one thing, he would not become a sheep shearer like his father. He joined the auxiliary schooner *Mardi Gras* at the age of fourteen as a deckhand. Ten years later when the vessel's owner and captain died of malaria he left the schooner to Duncan. By that time Duncan was an experienced navigator with a great knowledge of the Australian coast and the South Pacific islands. He demonstrated a somewhat strange sense of humour when he changed the name of the schooner from *Mardi Gras* to *Fat Tuesday*. His stated reason for doing so was that he couldn't stand funny foreign names and *Mardi Gras* and *Fat Tuesday* meant the same thing anyway so he couldn't see any problem.

18

It was October 15th 1945 when the six members of the salvage company finally assembled on board *Fat Tuesday*. The graceful auxiliary schooner that Derek remembered from before the war had undergone some drastic changes in the intervening years. Gone were the tall masts and billowing sails that he remembered and in their place were foreshortened masts and heavy lift derricks. The white hull was now painted warship grey and the accommodation had been expanded on the main deck. Her original engine had gone and a more powerful diesel was now the vessel's main means of propulsion. Previously the engine was the standby whilst the sails drove the ship from A to B. Now the roles were reversed. She still carried sails but they were rarely used.

Derek and his father stood on deck that first day discussing the changes.

'I knew from your letters that things

had changed but I never envisaged this', said Derek.

'You can't use sails in convoys,' replied Duncan Fitzpatrick.

'Convoys, you never mentioned convoys in your letters.'

'Several across to Port Moresby and others round to Darwin. In fact the government paid for a lot of the alterations. They were short of ships to move men and equipment.'

'What kind of equipment?' Derek asked.

'Field guns, trucks and even a couple of light tanks in addition to the men. On one trip to Moresby we carried four hundred troops on deck with all their gear.'

'Could you lift a bulldozer?'

'Sure, it can't be any heavier than a tank, but where's the dozer?'

'Stuck on a reef.'

'I can't take *Fat Tuesday* anywhere near a reef,' Duncan protested.

Derek began to explain about the stranded landing craft and its cargo and while he was doing so the pair were joined by the remainder of the group. In no time at all the discussion centred on the only means of getting the vehicles off the landing craft and on to the schooner. Once again they came to the same conclusion; they'd have to use a raft of some form. This time however, Duncan had the answer.

'I've used a raft on several occasions,' he said. 'I couldn't get close to the shore at times so I had to use a raft to unload heavy equipment. The dockyard made it and it's over there now. I can soon get hold of it again.'

'That's great news,' exclaimed Derek.

'Don't forget the batteries,' said Albert.

'Batteries, what kind?'

'Lead-acid and the heavy duty Nife type, we'll probably need both.'

'How many?'

'It's only guesswork but say half a dozen of each.'

Derek turned to his father again. 'Can we get those in the dockyard?' he asked.

'Probably, I'll let you know in the morning one way or the other.'

Four days later *Fat Tuesday* slipped her moorings and moved smoothly out to sea. On deck she carried the raft, whilst below decks were stowed batteries, tools, various motor engine spares and oxy-acetylene equipment. Altogether they had embarked sufficient dry and tinned stores to last approximately three months whilst they hoped to obtain sufficient fresh food from the islands they visited. The one addition that had been made to the personnel onboard was a cook, an elderly Chinese called Wong Kwee who had sailed on *Fat Tuesday* in the past. Duncan had no idea just how old Wong Kwee was and, if the truth be told, neither had the cook himself, however the meals he produced in the galley were classed as first rate. Inevitably the name Wong Kwee became abbreviated and after only a couple of days at sea he became affectionately known as Wonky.

Duncan Fitzpatrick knew his ship. He had at times acted as navigator, engineer and bosun and wasted no time at that first voyage in persuading the remainder of the men to follow his example. Accordingly Philip and Harry, whose specialisations were navigation and radio communications respectively, found themselves taking watches in the engine-room whilst Derek and Bill Toomey were given regular lessons in radio operation. Duncan's idea was that every member of the ship's complement should be able to take over any task in an emergency. The one exception to this rule was Wonky, his cooking was an art form and for any of them to even to attempt to emulate his work was felt to be impossible.

Under Bill Toomey's guidance all of them learnt how to handle deck winches and derricks and, when Duncan took over as tutor, to hoist and trim sails. They spent one morning drifting in mid-ocean while everyone took turns at raising and lowering the ship's lifeboat and dinghy. The lifeboat had an inboard engine whilst the dinghy had a small outboard. Once again everyone was given a basic instruction in boat handling. By the time *Fat Tuesday* nosed her way into the sheltered anchorage at Amatiki Island the six members of the salvage team had a basic idea of how most things worked aboard the vessel.

Once the schooner was safely anchored all eyes turned to the landing craft on the reef. It was obvious that the craft had moved in the intervening weeks since their last visit. Instead of sitting high and dry on the reef she now lay nose down as if slipping into the lagoon. They wasted no time at all in investigating the state of affairs aboard the landing craft. Derek, Duncan and Albert took the dinghy over to the stranded vessel. Derek was the first to scramble aboard and as he did so he felt movement from the metal hull beneath him. As Albert began to climb the rope ladder the movement became more pronounced. Derek leant over the side and called down to the others.

'Stay where you are for the time being, it feels as if she's about to slide off the reef. Let me check inside the hull.'

As he climbed down onto the vehicle deck Derek could see that a change had taken place since their last visit. The truck and jeeps appeared to be still secured in place but the bulldozer had broken free and had slid forward against the bow door. Also there was more water inside the hull. The blade of the bulldozer and almost half of the engine compartment was under water but because the vessel was lying nose down the remainder of the vehicles were dry. It seemed obvious to Derek after a careful inspection of the interior of the vessel that the extra water must have come from waves being thrown over the hull since he could find no damage that could allow water in.

As he clambered back down to the dinghy Derek could feel the vessel moving in a seesaw fashion, as if balanced precariously on a pivot. Duncan and he changed places and whilst Duncan climbed aboard Derek explained what he'd found to Albert.

'The dozer's broken free and is lying against the bow door. If we lower the ramp as things stand we'll probably lose the dozer.'

'From down here,' said Albert, 'it looked as if she's ready to float free. She's definitely been pushed a good ten feet across the reef from where she was.'

A few minutes later Duncan scrambled

back aboard. 'I think she'll float.' He said. 'Let's get back to the ship; I've got an idea that may work.'

Back onboard *Fat Tuesday* Duncan wasted no time in explaining his idea. With the aid of a quickly drawn sketch he outlined his plan.

'This is how I see it,' he said. 'There has obviously been some heavy weather since she ran aground originally. The rough seas appear to have pushed her almost across the reef and with a little help she could float free.'

'What kind of help?' Albert asked.

'A tow.'

'But if you try to tow her off you could well run *Fat Tuesday* aground.'

Duncan opened his sketch and pointing to it said, 'Not if we do it this way. If we put both forward anchors down and moor this ship stern on to the shore we can run a towing cable from our after winch. If we take the cable round the mooring bollards of that wrecked landing craft on the beach and then out to reef we should be able to pull her free.'

'She must be holed beneath the

waterline,' protested Harry. 'Surely she'll sink.'

'I can't see an alternative,' replied Duncan.

'What about our first idea of using the raft?' Bill asked.

'If we lower the ramp out there on the reef we'll lose the bulldozer because that has broken free and is resting against the ramp. We could also lose the rest because the very act of lowering the ramp could pull her off the reef. If that happens, the vehicle deck would flood.'

'So you believe that while the bow door is closed she'll have sufficient bouyancy to float if we can get her off the reef,' Derek said thoughtfully.

'I do.'

Derek looked around at the rest of the gathering. 'Do we got for it?' he asked.

Several heads nodded agreement.

It took most of the remainder of that day and the whole of the following morning to position the schooner and secure the towing hawser to the stranded landing craft. Whilst Duncan and Harry remained onboard the other four men took up positions either ashore or afloat. Philip and Albert were standing by the mooring bollards on the wrecked craft on the beach ready to signal for a halt in proceedings if anything should go wrong. Derek and Bill meanwhile were positioned, in the dinghy, well clear of the reef but close enough to observe any movement of the landing craft.

There was an air of tension amongst the six men as Duncan began to winch in the towing hawser. At first there was little to see but as the cable tightened and rose dripping from the sea the landing craft was seen to move slightly. It was a movement of the bow, swinging slowly to point directly at the beach. Then with little more than a slight screech of metal against coral the vessel slid clear of the reef. Duncan quickly increased the speed of the winch drum and reeled in the hawser as fast as he could. The freed craft behaved impeccably and grounded safely in two feet of water on the beach. By the time they had moored their salvaged vessel securely and recovered the towing cable it was sunset and little more could be done until the following day.

It took Albert most of the next morning to strip down the engine of the bulldozer and try to persuade it to start. Whilst he was busy with that job Philip and Harry were using the oxyacetylene torch on the chains that held the ramp in place. They had tried to release the ramp from what remained of the controls in the coxswain's position but that area was so badly damaged that it had proved impossible. In the meantime Derek and Bill had brought the raft ashore laden with the spare batteries.

With two of the fully charged heavy duty batteries from the ship replacing those from the bulldozer Albert attempted to start the reassembled engine. His first two attempts failed but the third time the engine exploded into action with a cloud of black smoke from its exhaust. That burst of noise drove birds and fruit bats screaming into the sky in protest. The cheering that followed it only served to infuriate the creatures more and it took some time for them to settle back into the trees.

By mid afternoon all four vehicles were standing on the beach. None of them had proved too difficult to start but nevertheless Albert was feeling extremely weary. He'd been working almost non-stop from first light so he was quite happy to sit back and let the others get on with transferring the machines from the beach to the schooner. Duncan knew his vessel well and he had decided to load the lorry first. It and the two jeeps would fit comfortably in the hold but the bulldozer was too big so it had to be secured on deck.

Duncan was using the lifeboat with its inboard engine to tow the raft to and from the ship. Albert sat in the shade of the damaged landing craft drinking a bottle of warm beer as first the lorry was ferried out and loaded and then the jeeps. When it was the turn of the bulldozer however the raft was almost awash and the lifeboat was struggling to tow its unwieldy charge. Derek took the dinghy with its outboard engine to assist and despite its small size it proved sufficient to guide the raft to the schooner. To

Albert watching from the shore those onboard seemed to take an inordinate time to prepare for lifting the machine but when the lift began he understood why. As soon as the bulldozer lifted clear of the raft the schooner heeled heavily to starboard and remained that way until the derricks swung the vehicle inboard.

With the exception of Duncan and Wonky the rest of the party spent the following day recovering the propellors from the three landing craft and every other piece of brass, copper and lead they could find. In addition to the pipework and fittings from the landing craft they also discovered a large quantity of spent artillery shell cases which they added to the growing pile of scrap metal. It was late afternoon and they had almost finished transferring the scrap to the ship when the first mortar shell landed in the sea close to the lifeboat.

Philip was on the tiller and he immediately swung the boat's head around and headed back towards the schooner and, as he did so, a second shell threw up a fountain of water astern. With

Philip in the boat was Harry, the pair had been returning to the beach to load the last of the scrap metal but now both of them were crouching low and urging the boat on towards safety. On board the schooner the remainder of the men had been stowing the recovered scrap in the hold but as soon as the sound of the first explosion was heard they hurried back on deck. Duncan screamed at them to get the engine started and the anchors recovered.

'What about the boat?' Derek shouted to his father.

'They can follow us out through the reef and we'll pick them up out there.'

The third shell fell between the boat and the schooner and it was then that Philip decided to take avoiding action by zigzagging. Ahead of him he could see the schooner getting underway and he took a chance and stood and waved towards the open sea. Two more fountains of water exploded from the sea but because of Philip's avoiding action they were well clear of the boat and by the time the sixth and seventh shells fell Philip was certain that they were out of range. Nevertheless he continued the avoiding manoeuvres until he was clear of the reef.

'Jesus, that was close,' exclaimed Philip after the boat had been recovered. 'I thought the war was over.'

'Obviously nobody told those buggers,' replied Derek.

'I presume they were Japanese,' Philip continued.

'Eight of the sods, they must have survived the fighting here.'

'I'll send a radio telegram reporting their presence,' said Duncan. 'However, we'd better be prepared for that sort of thing in future. Small groups of soldiers cut off from the outside world may well not know that the war is over.'

19

There were two other small islands in the same group as Amatiki, Taniela and Atuea. Taniela had been uninhabited until the American forces used it as a forward supply base for some months. Derek believed it was now unoccupied again. Atuea on the other hand was known to have had a small native population. Taniela was only two hours steaming away from Amatiki but Duncan had no intention of approaching the island until he'd conducted a preliminary survey. His idea was to approach the island in darkness with no lights showing onboard and to motor round it looking for any sign of life. Any light or fire on shore would stand out like a beacon against the dark of the land.

The six men held a conference on the bridge after their narrow escape from the Japanese on Amatiki. It was obvious to them all that the end of the war had given them a false sense of security. They had approached their first salvage operation in the belief that the Japanese forces had surrendered but they'd had a rude awakening. From now on caution had to be the watchword.

'Whenever we go ashore from now on we carry arms,' said Duncan.

'Have we got any?' Harry queried.

'Two 303s, does anyone know how to use them?'

Philip and Bill both said yes.

'Right, you two can give the others some lessons. There's plenty of ammunition. Until we can get that organised at least one of you will have to go ashore as guard.'

Duncan took the schooner on two complete circuits of Taniela without seeing one light from the shore. Nevertheless when the lifeboat was lowered the following morning he kept the ship underway. Philip and Harry took the boat inshore and met no opposition. They cautiously investigated what remained of the American army's presence and found little worth salvaging at first. In their initial investigation they found the remains of four Nissen huts that had been destroyed by fire and bombing. However, hidden behind the damaged huts they found a storage area holding oil drums of several types and sizes and most of them appeared to be full. A path of crushed coral led from there back to the beach about a hundred yards from where they had left the boat.

At that early stage in their salvage operations they had no means of communicating between the ship and shore other than by hand signals so the pair had to return to the ship to report what they had found. As soon as they described their finds Albert became extremely interested.

'Where there any identification marks on the drums?' He asked.

'There were a few marked highly inflammable but most of them were painted different colours,' replied Philip.

'What colours?'

'Blue, a lot of them were blue. There were some red ones and some of the smaller ones had letters and numbers on them.'

'Blue usually indicates diesel, red could be petrol and the smaller ones are probably lubricating oils.'

'How many are there?' asked Duncan.

'At least a hundred — probably more.'

'That's liquid gold,' exclaimed Duncan. 'I'll anchor as close inshore as I can and we'll get the raft in the water immediately.'

Altogether they recovered eighty-two drums of diesel, eleven of petrol and thirty-two smaller drums of various grades of lubricating oil. Each of the diesel and petrol drums held forty-five gallons and rolling them down to the beach and manhandling them onto the raft was exhausting work. It took them two full days but as a result they had sufficient fuel for the schooner's engine for many hundreds of miles of steaming.

Although both American and Japanese forces had landed on Atuea neither force had stayed and no fighting had taken place there. However, it was on that island that the salvage team recovered one of their greatest assets, a work-boat with a powerful engine that was to serve them well for the next few years. According to the island chief it had drifted ashore the previous year during the cyclone season. It was undamaged but was of no use to the islanders since they had no idea how to start the engine or fuel for it even if they had. After a short bout of bartering between Duncan and the chief, the boat was exchanged for a drum of paraffin, two sacks of rice and a case of tinned fish.

That first encounter with the native Pacific islanders was enough to demonstrate another shortcoming amongst the salvage team, only Duncan, and to a lesser extent Bill, was able to converse with the islanders. Duncan was fluent in Pidgin the only common language link between many of the islanders and the Pacific traders. Language lessons joined rifle practice as part of their daily routine.

Duncan had numerous contacts throughout the South Pacific region so he anticipated little difficulty in disposing of the salvaged vehicles but even he was surprised how quickly they were sold. Strictly speaking they should have been declared to the relevant authorities as salvage but it was decided that since no-one knew they had the vehicles it was pointless informing the authorities. A rendezvous was arranged at a quiet beach north of Brisbane. When *Fat Tuesday* dropped anchor a small group of men were seen to be waiting on the beach.

The bargaining took place onboard after the three men collected from the beach had inspected the vehicles. All four vehicles were sold together with the scrap metal and several drums of various fuel. The buyer claimed to be a building contractor and he paid in cash after everything was safely ashore. Bill Toomey, armed with one of the rifles, accompanied the bulldozer to the beach and remained there until the rest of the salvaged material had been landed and the cash handed over. The deal was conducted in U.S. dollars. All four vehicles were still on the beach when the schooner weighed anchor but several more men were seen to have joined the original three.

'They're planning to cut a track through the scrub with the dozer,' said Duncan.

'Where to?' Derek asked.

'There's a road about half a mile inland and they've got a low-loader waiting there to put the bulldozer on.'

'Where are we going?'

'Just a few miles up the coast, out of their sight.'

'Don't you trust them?'

'Let's say I'm being cautious, afterall you don't find many legitimate building contractors who can produce that amount of ready cash in so short a time.'

That evening with the schooner safely anchored in a quiet cove the six men held a celebratory meeting. After a sum to cover the operating costs of the schooner had been set aside the balance of the salvage money was divided equally between them. Harry counted his money several times, did a couple of sums and finally declared in an astonished tone that he had received the equivalent of one years' wages for four weeks work.

'It was a great start but we can't expect it to be so easy in future,' said Derek.

'I agree,' declared Duncan. 'This time there was no competition and the pickings were good but you can't count on it being like that for very long.'

'What do you suggest we do next then?' Albert asked.

'We need a genuine reason for visiting populated islands especially those with operational military bases so I was thinking of resuming normal trading and doing the salvage work as and when opportunities arise.'

'Yes,' said Philip thoughtfully. 'I think that makes sense.'

Duncan looked around at the men gathered in the messroom. 'Are we all in agreement?' He asked.

Five men nodded in reply.

'Where do we start?' Bill asked.

'Brisbane,' said Duncan. 'We'll see if we can pick up a cargo there.'

Two days later they were loading a small amount of mixed cargo destined for Port Vila and the Fijian port of Suva. There wasn't enough cargo to make a profit on the passage but Duncan was quite happy to take it as it gave him the opportunity to make the islanders aware that he was back in business. However, their plans were altered when the Royal Australian Navy in the shape of a Lieutenant Commander Corrigan intervened. He strolled along the quayside and stood surveying *Fat Tuesday* for some minutes before calling to Duncan, 'Is Captain Fitzpatrick aboard?'

'That's me,' replied Duncan.

'May I come aboard Captain?'

'Yes, please do so.'

A few minutes later the pair was settled in Duncan's cabin.

'I understand you are loading cargo for the islands Captain.'

'Yes, I'm trying to re-establish the trade I had before the war. We're currently loading cargo for Port Vila and Suva.'

'Is it urgently required there?'

'No, it's just routine stuff. Why do you ask?'

'We have medical supplies that are urgently needed in Port Moresby, can you take them?'

'Surely urgent medicines can be flown in,' replied Duncan.

'Ah, you misunderstand me. I should have said medical equipment. It's actually a prefabricated building which when assembled forms a fully fitted surgical unit.'

'I see, then the answer is yes, we'll take it.'

'There is more,' said Corrigan. 'We've also got stores for Honiara and we'd like a liaison team lifting off Atoll 437.'

'Honiara's okay but I don't know Atoll 437. Where is it?'

Corrigan opened his briefcase and produced a folded sheet of paper. 'The Americans provided this,' he said. He unfolded the paper to reveal a hand drawn sketch of the atoll. 'Latitude and longitude and approach details for the anchorage,' he continued, pointing to the sketch.

Duncan walked through to the wheel-house and returned a few minutes later with a large-scale chart of the South Pacific. Taking the sketch he compared it with the chart. After a short while he said, 'It seems to me that the obvious route would be Port Moresby, Honiara, Atoll 437 then down to Fiji, across to Port Vila and back here. How big is this liaison team?'

'Just six men, you could land them in Fiji and they can get a flight back here.'

'Okay,' said Duncan. 'I'll need the dimensions, weights etc of your cargo.'

Corrigan took another sheet of paper from his briefcase and handed it over without comment. Duncan studied it, made a couple of calculations in pencil and then nodded his head. 'How soon can you get it here?' He asked.

'The lorries are waiting at the end of the quay,' said Corrigan with a smile.

'You were pretty sure of yourself,' replied Duncan.

'No, I travelled more in hope than certainty. There is one more thing,' he muttered producing yet more paper from his case. 'You might find these useful if you have to call at any other islands. They're in Japanese explaining that the war is over. Apparently there are thousands of their troops who have no idea it's finished.'

Duncan smiled as he took the handful of leaflets. 'They could be useful,' he agreed.

20

I didn't know enough about the laws of salvage to say that what Albert and his companions were doing was illegal so I refrained from mentioning that particular point when I explained to Jennifer what I'd found in the notes. However, in my mind I was fairly certain that they were bending the salvage laws with that first recovery operation and the subsequent sale of the vehicles.

We were sitting together out on deck as I was telling her about the first mention of Atoll 437, or the Kingston Islands as Albert subsequently referred to them. When I was explaining the route that they took via Port Moresby and Honiara she stopped me.

'I can't visualise these places,' she said. 'Can you show me them on a chart?'

Joe was on the wheel so I asked him for a large-scale chart of the South Pacific. He handed me the wheel and went below to find one. He was back a few minutes later.

'I've left it on the chart table, I'll put it away later when you've finished.'

Bending over the chart table a few minutes later with Jennifer close beside me I found it extremely hard to concentrate on what I was supposed to be showing her. Out on deck her shorts and bikini top seemed perfectly normal attire but down below, standing shoulder to shoulder at the chart table, I found it to be extreemely distracting, particularly so as she bent to study the chart.

'One of the first things you have to remember when reading your grandfather's notes is that things have changed somewhat since he wrote them.'

'In what way?' Jennifer asked.

'Well for one thing most of these island nations have become independent since the war. Part of what we now call Indonesia used to be the Dutch East Indies, Papua New Guinea used to be administered by the Australians, it was known as Papua and New Guinea.'

'Okay, I'll bear that in mind. Now show

222

me Port Moresby and the rest of those places you mentioned.'

I showed her the route taken by the schooner from Brisbane north to Port Moresby, then across to Honiara in the Solomon Islands, north to Atoll 437, south to Suva in Fiji and finally steering west to Port Vila in Vanuatu before returning to Brisbane.

'Fiji has always been Fiji hasn't it?' Jennifer asked.

'Yes I think so.'

'What about Vanuatu?'

'It used to be a condominium called the New Hebrides.'

'A what?'

'A condominium; that means it was administered by two nations, the British and the French at the same time.'

'Good grief, did they ever agree on anything?'

I do remember laughing at that. 'I'm told it was often referred to as a pandemonium rather than a condominium. Does that answer your question?' I replied.

'Yes, I think I can imagine what a shambles the administration would be.

How far have you got with the note-books?'

'I'm about halfway through them.'

'Have you found any mention of Valerie yet?'

'No, none at all.'

'May I see what's left?'

'Of course.'

I led the way into my cabin and whilst I was busy retrieving the notebooks from the far side of the bed Jennifer was settling herself on it. As I passed the unread books across to her a slip of white paper fell from one onto her lap. When she picked it up she gave a gasp of surprise. Turning the paper over she revealed a photograph, another picture of a smiling young woman. Across the bottom corner were written the words, 'With love Valerie.'

'She's beautiful,' said Jennifer as she handed the photograph to me.

'I agree she was beautiful,' I replied, emphasising the word was.

'Was?' Jennifer muttered. Then, as she remembered the photograph the Americans had taken she said, 'Yes, of course,

I'd forgotten.' She took the photograph back from me and studied it more thoroughly. 'That looks like a nurse's uniform she's wearing. I wonder where they met.'

'Well, the answer is probably somewhere in here,' I said holding up the bundle of notebooks.

'I think I'd better change my mind and read through those with you. We'll probably find her story faster that way. Let's take them through to the saloon there'll be more room to work there.'

We sat side by side at the saloon table with the notebooks and diaries piled in front of us. I had tried to sort them into date order but because of Albert's later additions and alterations there was no way I could be certain that they were in the correct order. I attempted to concentrate on the book I'd been reading the night before but the proximity of the half-naked girl beside me was too distracting. It came to a head when she reached across me to take the next book and her breast pressed against my right arm. I think I groaned aloud.

'It's no good, Jenny,' I said. 'I cannot concentrate with you beside me. You'll either have to leave me to it or put some more clothes on.'

'There is a third alternative,' she said, pressing even closer to me.

'There is?'

She lifted her head and kissed me lightly on the lips. 'Yes, you could help me take these off.'

I was stunned, but it didn't take me long to recover. As for not mixing business and pleasure I completely forgot about it. Our relationship as employer and employee was destroyed that day. It changed to that of lovers. Kesa must have known what was happening because she never disturbed us by announcing dinner that evening. As for the notebooks, I found them neatly arranged in my cabin again the next morning.

There was a certain inevitability about what happened that day. Jennifer and I had become very close in Fiji but we hadn't taken that final step then. I was the one who'd backed away because of my ideas about business and pleasure but

Jennifer had finally broken down my defences. Don't get me wrong, I was delighted that she had done so. If she hadn't made that first move I probably would have done so eventually. I'd certainly fantasised enough about it but my idea had been to leave it until we returned to England. In my minds eye I had visualised a fine meal, soft lights, and music but instead the sensuous nature of the tropics and sensual nature of the girl overwhelmed me.

It was two days before either of us was able to concentrate on the notebooks again and when we did so we found the first mention of Valerie within minutes of starting work. She boarded the schooner in Port Moresby as a convalescent passenger bound for Brisbane. Her two-year stint as a nursing sister at a military hospital had come to an end when she suffered a debilitating attack of malaria. The doctor who drove her down to the ship said she was badly in need of a rest cure and he felt that the voyage via the Solomon Islands and Fiji would be ideal.

During the passage from Port Moresby

to Honiara on Guadalcanal little was seen of the nurse. She took her meals in her cabin and appeared on deck only in the cool of the evening. However, once they had sailed from Honiara she began to appear for meals in the saloon and spend more time on deck during the day.

'I've read this section through a couple of times but I can't see why she should spend so much time in her cabin at first,' said Jennifer.

'Could be any one of a number of things,' I replied.

'Such as?'

'Seasickness or simply being so tired by her illness that she needed sleep.'

'That's possible I suppose, but it doesn't explain why she suddenly started spending more time on deck during the day.'

'Albert was working on deck after they sailed from Honiara.'

'He was?'

'Yes, look here, you've skipped over this section because he was writing about vehicles but that's why he was on deck so much.'

At the end of the jetty where the schooner had berthed in Honiara was a dump of damaged vehicles. Albert had strolled along there to see if there was anything worth salvaging. He was surprised to find several trucks and jeeps that he felt could be cannibalised to make working vehicles. While he was examining one of the jeeps an American soldier approached him.

'You looking for something bud?'

'I was wondering why this lot is here,' replied Albert.

'It's just a load of scrap. We're probably going to dump the lot at sea.'

'Dump it? Can I take some of these off your hands?'

'I expect so. Just have a word with the Sergeant, that's his office over there.'

When they sailed from Honiara they carried eight damaged jeeps on deck.

21

Albert and Duncan had discussed the removal of the jeeps with the Sergeant in Honiara. During that meeting Duncan took the opportunity to ask about the remainder of the scrap vehicles. He was particularly interested in half a dozen trucks that Albert had identified for possible cannibalisation. The Sergeant had readily agreed to the removal of the jeeps but when he saw their interest in the trucks he began to see the possibility of making money. However, Duncan was reluctant to commit to any expenditure for scrap vehicles other than those suitable for reconstruction, whilst the Sergeant wanted every damaged machine removing no matter what its condition. No agreement was reached before *Fat Tuesday* had to continue her voyage.

They sailed at first light from Honiara and headed across Iron Bottom Sound for the passage between the islands of

Santa Isabel and Malaita. Working beneath an awning rigged over the foredeck Albert and Harry began the reconstruction of the first of the jeeps. They spread a large tarpaulin on the deck and positioned two of the vehicles side by side on top of it.

Superficially the first of the jeeps appeared to be in good condition. However, two neat round holes in the bonnet led to an internal shambles. The engine block was completely shattered. The second machine had certainly seen better days, everything behind the driver's seat was badly crushed but its engine was in perfect condition. Using a jury-rigged block and tackle the damaged engine was lifted clear of its machine, stripped of any usable parts then dropped over the side. One hour later the good engine from the other jeep had replaced it. In less than a morning the two men had constructed a usable machine. The engine had sounded a bit rough when they first tested it but after twenty minutes of fine-tuning they had it running smoothly.

The two men were standing back admiring their work when Valerie brought them a drink. 'What will you do with it now?' She asked.

'Once we've given it a test run it'll be for sale,' replied Albert.

'When will you be able to test it out?'

'It'll probably be when we reach Suva. Our next stop is at that American base on the atoll and we're anchoring there so we'll have to wait until Suva, assuming of course that we get alongside the jetty there.'

Harry left them at that point leaving Albert and Valerie standing in the shade of the awning.

'We might as well be comfortable,' said Albert indicating the two seats in the jeep.

'Good idea,' replied Valerie as she seated herself behind the steering wheel.

'You look at home there. Have you driven a car before?'

Valerie smiled. 'Cars, tractors and more recently ambulances, I used to help my father and my brother when they were servicing their vehicles. I've been itching to help you all morning.'

'Well you can help me strip the usable bits off that wreck before we dump it over the side,' said Albert indicating what remained of the other jeep. 'It'll be a messy job though so you won't be able to wear that dress.'

Valerie gave a chuckle. 'Give me ten minutes I've got some old clothes I can change into.'

Up on the bridge wing Derek and Duncan had been watching the pair on the foredeck.

'That's the first time I've seen that girl smiling since she came aboard,' remarked Duncan.

'This voyage has done her good,' Derek replied. 'She was one step away from complete collapse when she came aboard.'

'Albert's looking happy as well.'

'That's probably the first woman he's laughed with since his wife died.'

'I didn't know he'd been married.'

'Yes, married with one youngster. When she was killed in the bombing he gave the baby to his sister-in-law. He sends money home for the boy's upkeep.'

'How do you know all that, he never talks about family in the mess?' Duncan said.

'We got drunk together on VE day.'

'Where does he come from?'

'A place called Hull, one of the major ports in England. It was badly bombed. Albert lost his wife, his parents and his home in one night.'

'Poor bastard,' said Duncan as he moved away from the rail. 'Let's leave them in peace to enjoy each other's company.'

A few minutes later Valerie left the foredeck only to reappear shortly afterwards dressed in a pair of khaki shorts and shirt. In her absence Albert had studied what remained of the battered jeep and had decided to remove the front axle and wheels after stripping any usable instruments from the dashboard. He had an idea that the axle would be needed for one of the other scrap jeeps. Valerie started work on the instruments whilst Albert assessed the next vehicle for reconstruction.

The pair worked side by side throughout the afternoon pausing only for the occasional drink. By the time the loss of daylight brought their work to an end the remnants of the battered jeep had been dropped over the side and considerable progress had been made in the restoration of another of the vehicles. As he gathered up the tools and stowed them in the back of the machine they had been working on Albert looked across at Valerie. Her hands were black with oil, her shirt and shorts were liberally daubed with it and a black streak adorned her face.

'You're not a bad mechanic Valerie,' he said.

She gave a shy smile. 'You're not so bad yourself,' she replied.

That day set a pattern for the remainder of the week with the two of them working alongside each other restoring the wrecks. Whenever extra hands or muscle were required then Harry or Bill came to their assistance but otherwise the pair worked together in close companionship. The understanding that began to develop between them was at times almost psychic. One or the other would reach for a particular tool only to find that it was already being held out to them. At other times when they were considering which was the best way to solve a particular problem they both came to the same conclusion at the same time. It was inevitable therefore that their relationship would become closer as the voyage continued.

One habit that had developed amongst those aboard the schooner was for those not on duty to gather on the foredeck after the evening meal. Harry once described these get-togethers as 'chinwag time' but in effect they were a chance to exchange ideas and any news on the events of the day. At the meeting on the night before their arrival at the American Atoll Albert announced that the work on the jeeps was almost complete.

'How many are operational?' Duncan asked.

'Three are in full working order and there are two more that only need a few extra bits and pieces.' Albert replied.

'You mean that if we get those bits we'll have five vehicles for sale.'

Albert nodded. 'I was wondering if we might find what we need tomorrow,' he said.

'Make out a list and I'll do my best for you if I get ashore. All we've got to do at the Atoll is to collect the liaison team so we may not anchor.'

At first light the next day *Fat Tuesday* cautiously approached the buoyed channel leading to the anchorage. A launch from the American base came out to meet them but no attempt was made to board the schooner. The one man aboard the launch signalled them to follow him into the lagoon and to drop anchor. Duncan had positioned Bill in the bows to act as leadsman but the water inside the lagoon was so still and clear that the leadline wasn't required. Twenty minutes after entering the lagoon the schooner was safely anchored.

The American launch had stayed close by whilst the schooner completed the anchoring manoeuvre. The coxswain then brought it alongside and called out that his orders were to conduct the captain ashore. A few minutes later Duncan was on his way. The remainder of the ship's company gathered on the bridge and began to examine the atoll through binoculars.

What they saw was an almost circular atoll consisting of two islands connected by a bridge to the north and west and, completing the circle to the south and east, a continuous coral reef. The only gap in the circle being the one through which the schooner had entered the lagoon. The larger of the two islands was completely flat with no vegetation whatsoever. In complete contrast was the second island's lush tropical growth, beneath and amongst which stood several substantial prefabricated buildings and a number of water and fuel tanks. Lined up by the bridge were two bulldozers, a fire truck and three or four smaller vehicles. Several small craft lay alongside a wooden jetty, the jetty where Duncan had landed.

At first there appeared to be little movement onshore. Occasionally men could be seen moving around but only at a leisurely pace. However, about an hour after Duncan's departure a sudden burst of activity around the jetty caught their attention. They could see a small crane being used to lower various crates and cases into a barge. Bill watched that loading operation for a few minutes before calling Harry to assist him in preparing the deck winch and derricks.

'We might as well be ready for them,' he said. 'It looks as if that liaison team has quite a bit of heavy gear.'

Whilst the activity continued around the barge, the launch brought Duncan back to the schooner. As soon as he was aboard again he called everyone together to explain what was about to happen.

'We've arrived a day earlier than they were expecting so they've still some packing up to do. There's a six man Australian team to be landed in Fiji with all their gear but I've also agreed to take some Americans.'

'How many?' asked Philip.

'Two men but there's also a quantity of equipment for onward shipment to the States.'

'Are we landing them in Fiji as well?'

'Yes. Their regular supply ship was due here last week but she's still tied up elsewhere and they were due to leave on that.'

Bill pointed to the activity ashore. 'Is

that the equipment they're loading now?'

'Some of it is for offloading in Fiji but some of it is for us. They've agreed to let us have some surplus vehicle spares in return for us landing their men in Fiji. Apparently the whole base is being run down prior to decommissioning so there's a fair bit of stuff they want rid of.'

'Don't they have to account for the spares?' asked Albert.

'Vehicle spares are classed as consumables.'

'What, all of them?'

'That's what they told me.'

'What else do they want rid of?' Harry asked.

'I don't know yet, but I have agreed with the base commander to return here on our next trip. He says he'll make it worth our while.'

They sailed for Fiji later that day.

22

Jennifer and I had become so involved with, and so distracted by, each other that we neglected Albert's notebooks for some time. However, when Joe announced at breakfast one morning that we were only two days from the Kingston Islands we both realised that we had to return to them. It was that morning shortly after we'd resumed our reading that I came to understand that we would never know the full extent of Albert's activities.

'There are a lot of gaps, Jenny.' I said, putting down the notebook I'd been reading.

'Gaps?'

'Yes, for example, when they recovered the bulldozer from that landing craft it was late in 1945. This book details their arrival in Fiji and the sale of the first of the repaired jeeps but according to this it's now the middle of 1946.'

'Well it was a long voyage, Brisbane,

PNG, the Solomons and then the Atoll before Fiji.'

'Yes, that's true but I still think he's left gaps in the story.'

'He's probably left out the more mundane bits,' replied Jennifer. 'There are things though that I find it hard to come to terms with.'

'What do you mean?'

'Well there's the casual way that they dispose of unwanted bits of those jeeps by tossing them over the side.'

'I don't suppose it even occurred to them that they were doing anything wrong. Albert in particular had seen many thousands of tons of shipping sent to the bottom during the war. That was pollution on a major scale.'

Despite the missing sections in Albert's narrative I had begun to tie some events together. In Fiji Mr Patel had told us about the purchase of a jeep, a jeep with two holes in the bonnet, and I'd just read about it. Other things were also beginning to slot into place. We'd found the first mention of Valerie, and Atoll 437 was definitely what Albert had renamed the

Kingston Islands. Although when he'd decided to rename them was still a mystery.

As I read on I could see a regular pattern emerging in both the route taken by *Fat Tuesday* and by the salvage work undertaken by her crew. I never found any reference to an agreement between the American forces in Honiara and Duncan and his fellow crew members but nevertheless trucks began to appear amongst the salvaged vehicles. It also became apparent that as the American forces on the atoll began to be reduced in number *Fat Tuesday* and her crew began to spend more and more time there. The large trucks were too difficult to strip down onboard the ship so they were being ferried from Honiara to the atoll and being worked on there.

For a while the only references I could find of Valerie after that first voyage occurred whenever the ship returned to Australia. Valerie had resumed her nursing career in a Brisbane hospital. She and Albert met for a few days every two or three months but in his notes Albert made no mention of romance. However, they married in a civil ceremony early in 1947. Shortly afterwards Valerie joined *Fat Tuesday* as a permanent member of the crew.

A lot happened in the early months of that year both on the American base and aboard *Fat Tuesday*. On the atoll the Americans began the run-down of personnel in earnest. In the space of a few weeks the majority had been evacuated leaving only a handful of men to finalise the de-storing of the base. Those that remained appeared to have done little work judging by the stores and other equipment that were abandoned when they finally left. However, one aspect of their normal duties that hadn't been forgotten was the daily trundle up and down the runway by the bulldozer. This was to ensure that nothing was allowed to grow through the crushed coral of the landing strip that could impede an aircraft landing. That bulldozer was left at the side of the runway when the last troops departed.

Shortly after the atoll was finally abandoned by the Americans Albert and

Valerie took up residence there. Judging by Albert's notes he and Valerie lived on the islands for months at a time and worked at restoring vehicles delivered there by the schooner. At times they appeared to have the islands to themselves for weeks then, at other times, the schooner would be visiting every few days, ferrying scrap metal and vehicles to and fro. On one such visit Albert noted that the schooner's hold was packed with scrap metal of every conceivable kind — shell-cases, brass and copper pipework, aero engines, ship's propellers and even a small Japanese tank. In addition the schooner carried four restored trucks on deck when she sailed.

Late in 1947, whilst Albert and Valerie were living on the islands, two American carrier aircraft flew low over the runway. They actually made several passes over the islands before gaining height and flying off towards the west. Thinking the aircraft were intending to land Albert had hurried down to the runway and raised the arrestor wires. Because the runway was so short it had been equipped like an aircraft carrier with an arrangement of arrestor wires to bring the planes to a halt before they ran out of runway and finished in the sea. All carrier-borne aircraft were fitted with a hook under the fuselage to catch onto those wires.

Seeing Albert's action one of the aircraft flew low and slow past him whilst the pilot indicated with hand signals that they had no intention of landing. Nevertheless, after that incident Albert ran the bulldozer up and down the runway once a week and kept the arrestor gear well maintained. The wires were raised and lowered by one hand-operated lever positioned by the runway but it required frequent applications of lubricating oil for smooth operation.

I smiled to myself when I read about the arrestor wires. The very mention of them brought back memories of my time in the navy. In my mind's eye I could see the pilots in the mess room belting out the words of one of their favourite songs:-

They say in the Air Force a landing's okay.

If the pilot gets out and can still
*   walk away.*
But in the Fleet Air Arm the pros-
*   pects are grim*
If the landing's piss-poor and the
*   pilot can't swim.*

In the time that Albert and his wife lived on the islands their living expenses were virtually nil. The departing Americans had left large quantities of dried and tinned food and a garden that produced all manner of fruit and vegetables. They had abundant water since the islands had been equipped with enough rainwater tanks to supply a garrison of some two hundred men and their electricity supply came from a motor generator.

Throughout this period both Albert's and Valerie's shares of the salvage money were being deposited in a Fijian branch of an Australian bank. Without either of them being consciously aware of it their combined earnings were mounting up to what for them was a small fortune. Albert was still sending money home to support his son but the amount was so small that it was barely making a dent in his bank balance. He had based the remittance on his wartime salary and had never adjusted it.

Early in 1948 a chance encounter with a group of native fishermen on a small island off New Guinea led to a strange discovery. On this occasion both Albert and Valerie were aboard the schooner having been back to Brisbane for a brief visit.

According to Albert's notes the schooner had anchored off the island for the crew to investigate the wreckage of a small ship lying partly submerged on the beach. However, before they had launched a boat a native canoe made its way out to *Fat Tuesday*. The three men aboard the canoe had fish, coconuts and pawpaw for sale. Duncan signalled for them to come aboard. There followed a protracted bout of bartering in pidgin that Albert for one struggled to follow. The upshot was that the natives' offerings were exchanged for rice and a can of kerosene.

Taking the opportunity to make use of

their local knowledge Duncan began to question the fishermen about the wreck and any other wartime remains on the island. The reply he received was so odd that he asked for it to be repeated.

'Pinas long ain rot,' said the man, pointing along the beach.

Then in response to Duncan's next question replied, 'Longwe lik lik.'

'What did he say?' Albert asked.

'He said that there's a motor boat on an iron road someway along the beach.'

'Surely you've missed something in the translation.'

'No, he said it twice, but I've no idea what he means by an iron road.'

'How far is it?'

'Longwe lik lik, or if you like, not near not far. The concept of distance is not easy to explain in pidgin.'

There followed another burst of pidgin from the older of the fishermen that was accompanied by much arm waving. The word 'tambu' was repeated frequently. Eventually Duncan and the fisherman appeared to reach some form of agreement.

'He's going to show us where it is but he won't go near it because he says it's taboo to him and his people.' Duncan said.

'I thought I understood pidgin but I can't understand half of what he says,' complained Albert.

'That's because he's mixing pidgin and his place-talk. I'm having difficulty at times as well but I think I've got the general gist of what he's been saying. He wants us to put a boat in the water and follow his canoe.'

Half an hour later the boat carrying Duncan, Bill and Albert lay stopped off a beach. The fisherman had pointed to the shore before turning his canoe and hurrying off in the reverse direction. Duncan examined the shoreline through binoculars.

'Can't see a damned thing,' he muttered. 'If there's a boat there it must be well hidden.'

He nodded to Albert to put the engine in gear and turned the boat's head towards the beach. As they got nearer they could see a break in the tree-line but nothing else. It wasn't until they stepped onto the beach that they discovered the 'iron road' that the native fisherman had told them about. It was almost hidden in the sand and Bill Toomey found it by tripping over it.

'Good grief,' he exclaimed, 'it's a bloody railway track.'

The track led across the narrow beach and into the dense tropical undergrowth. After stumbling along it, pushing aside the encroaching greenery, they came to a large cave entrance. A few feet inside they could see the bow of a small landing craft. It was sitting on a wheeled trolley astride the railway track. Signalling the others to wait, Duncan ventured further into the gloom of the cavern. He stood for some time allowing his eyes to adjust to the dim light before returning to the others.

'This cave goes back a long way. There's another boat behind this one but I can't see any further. We need torches and tools before we do any more exploring.'

'Our people found something like this

in Rabaul,' said Bill.

'Why go to all this trouble?' asked Albert.

'If it can't be seen, it can't be bombed,' replied Bill.

23

Duncan decided to move the schooner to an anchorage close to the 'iron road'. He had to proceed with caution because although there was no evidence of a reef there were a number of scattered coral heads that could easily have torn a hole in the hull. They eventually anchored within a hundred yards of the shore on a secure sandy bottom.

On that first day they explored the cave environs carefully before moving into the cave itself. Duncan allowed only two men at a time into the interior and they had specific orders to check and recheck before moving any object. They had learnt in the short time they had been working together that abandoned equipment from both sides of the conflict had sometimes been booby-trapped. On this occasion however, no booby traps were found in the vicinity of the landing craft. What they did find was a diesel generator connected to a switchboard. It appeared to supply electricity to a lighting system that ran throughout the cavern.

It took Albert two days to persuade the generator to produce light and whilst he was working on that the others were busy assessing the condition of the landing craft and clearing the overgrown railway track. It was obvious to them all that the cave extended much further back into the hillside than the section housing the boats and the generator but it seemed sensible to wait for proper lighting before venturing into the unknown.

Both landing craft appeared to be relatively new and in good condition. Although they could only carry about twenty men in addition to the crew they were exceptionally well equipped. Each had a small but well fitted galley, bunks for a crew of six and an enclosed wheelhouse. Their armament was still in place — two heavy machine-guns sited above the wheelhouse. Albert estimated that their engines would drive them along at around twelve knots and possibly even faster in an emergency. This type of craft had been used by the Japanese forces to patrol the islands because they could operate in shallow waters and because of their ability to carry small groups of soldiers to any trouble spots in a hurry.

Albert was against testing the engines of the two craft whilst they were *in situ* because of the build up of carbon monoxide from the exhaust gases. There was also the possibility that the vibration from the engine could cause the vessels to shift on the trolleys. Launching them was straightforward. A cable ran from the trolley back to an electric winch. By merely releasing the brake on the winch drum the trolley carrying the first of the landing craft began to roll slowly down the railway track. The speed of launching was controlled by applying the brake intermittently — this slowed the vessel until it entered the water and floated free from its trolley. Once in the water it was towed out to where the schooner lay at anchor and secured alongside her. In order to launch the second vessel the cable had to be rewound after the first trolley had been lifted bodily from the track.

With the pair of landing craft secured alongside *Fat Tuesday*, Albert and Valerie were left to test the engines whilst the remainder of the group began the exploration of the cave system. What they discovered astounded them. A series of man-made tunnels linked caves used as storage areas and living quarters. Two vertical shafts led up to gun emplacements that overlooked the beach and the schooner. Here heavy machine guns and mortars were still in place. In the living quarters a series of bunks held neatly folded bedding and tables were littered with eating utensils. One storage area was packed with ammunition of various kinds whilst another held tinned and dried foodstuffs.

'It's like a land version of the *Marie Celeste*,' said Harry.

'I can understand why those fishermen said it was taboo,' muttered Philip. 'There is a spooky feel to the place. Where did they all go?'

They were interrupted then by the

arrival of Derek and Bill who had been investigating a narrow side tunnel.

'Two of them didn't go anywhere,' said Derek. 'There are two bodies back there, Japanese officers who appear to have committed hari kari.'

'It was bloody frightening,' added Bill. 'We heard noises just before we found the bodies. It gave me quite a turn. The room they are in looks like their quarters but the noises were coming from a room inside theirs.'

'There was a radio room and the noises were coming from a radio receiver, it must be powered by the same generator as the lights. It was quite a shock hearing noises and finding bodies almost simultaneously.'

Harry looked around nervously. 'Come on,' he said. 'I've had enough of this place, let's get back aboard.'

That evening onboard *Fat Tuesday* the discussion centred on the two landing craft. There were two main schools of thought and opinions varied on which of the two to follow. The first was simply to find a buyer for them, the second to make use of them themselves. Gradually as all the pros and cons were discussed opinions began to swing more and more in favour of option two. They all knew that the salvage side of their operation was decreasing whilst the demand for trade was increasing. It seemed logical therefore to utilise these smaller vessels as feeder for the schooner. Eventually, late in the night, they reached a consensus — they would keep the two craft and use them to expand their trading routes.

The following morning they began to convert the vessels from men-of-war to innocent trading vessels. Whilst Albert was busy running up and testing the engines others were unshipping the machine guns and their mounts. Bill Toomey was working in the schooner's paint locker searching out every can of paint he could find whilst Derek and Harry were on a similar mission ashore.

It took them almost a week to finish the conversion. Being flat-bottomed the landing craft could be safely beached and once beached work began to paint the hulls. Using a mixture of paint from the schooner and the Japanese stores the hull colour was changed from dark grey to green whilst the wheelhouses were painted white. Both vessels were given names and became *Tuesday One* and *Tuesday Two*. Valerie was given the honour of naming them and in lieu of Champagne, used bottles of saki liberated from the Japanese stores.

All week they had deliberated on where to base the two vessels. In the end they decided on Honiara in the Solomon Islands. On their previous visits there they had often been approached to deliver trade goods to one or more of the many smaller islands in the group. This had often proved impossible for them because of the size of the schooner and the shallow waters around the islands. Honiara also offered the possibility of hiring local crew from amongst men who had been trained by the American forces and who were now finding themselves out of work as the bases were being decommissioned.

Ten days after the discovery of the landing craft the three vessels sailed in company for Honiara. Aboard *Tuesday One* were Philip and Harry whilst *Tuesday Two* was manned by Derek and Bill. The thirty-six hour passage passed off without incident. In Honiara Derek and Harry were selected to remain with the landing craft to find suitable crews and set up trading links. Three islanders were hired as crew for *Fat Tuesday* to replace them.

Although the emphasis of the company was switching from salvage to trade there were still a number of loose ends to be cleared up at the atoll. Albert and Valerie were landed there again because there were several trucks and a couple of jeeps awaiting repair. One of the reasons they had returned to Brisbane on the previous trip had been to purchase vehicle spares of the type they required. Buyers were already waiting in Suva for two of the trucks to be delivered and Duncan delayed his departure from their island base until they were available.

Duncan estimated that the round trip from the atoll to Suva and back would take about ten days. His plan was to make as fast a passage as possible leaving Albert and Valerie to work on the remaining vehicles. Once back at the islands those vehicles would be loaded and Albert and Valerie would rejoin the crew of the schooner. Their atoll base was to be abandoned.

24

I started reading the next volume of Albert's diary the day before our arrival at the atoll and soon began to realise that what I was reading was nothing like what had gone before. It was so different in fact that I decided to quote his diary entries verbatim.

March 21st 1948 — written in July.

Valerie and I had completed the work on the trucks and had packed up most of our tools ready for loading onto the schooner. We were expecting Duncan to return in two or three days from his visit to Suva. Having lived on the islands for months at a time we'd become used to the sounds of the trade winds blowing through the trees and the hiss of the surf on the reef so any unusual sound was easy to pick up. Valerie heard it first; I saw her head come up sharply as she peered into the sky searching for the source of the unusual note. I heard it shortly afterwards, an aero engine misfiring and growing louder by the second.

The aircraft came in low from the sea almost at stalling speed. It dropped tiredly onto the end of the runway and with brakes squealing in protest stopped a few feet short of the sea at the other end. I was running before the plane landed thinking that the arrestor wires would be needed but I was too late and in any case the aircraft wasn't military and didn't have an arrestor book. Behind me I heard Valerie start up one of the repaired jeeps so I slowed down and waited until she reached me. By the time we got to the aircraft the pilot was already on the ground and a second man dropped from the machine as we arrived.

The pilot introduced himself as Brad and his companion as Lee. From his accent I judged Brad to be American his co-pilot was, I believe, Japanese. From the beginning they made it plain that they didn't want us anywhere near *their machine. In fact I got the impression that they didn't want us anywhere near them at all. When I suggested that they hitch a lift with us on Fat Tuesday Brad refused point blank. He was adamant that he would fly his aircraft from the island despite its short runway. I volunteered my services as an engineer but received a blunt, thanks but no thanks, in reply. The only help they wanted was the loan of a ladder and a table — a ladder to reach the engine and a table for their tools and spares. Lee came with us in the jeep to collect those.*

While we were loading the jeep Valerie suggested to Lee that she make up a couple of beds in one of the huts for them. His response was as brusque as his companion's. 'Sleep in plane' he said. He virtually commandeered the jeep, parking it beside the plane that night and using it twice the next day to collect food and water from us. Throughout that second day Valerie and I watched as the two men worked on the plane but it was almost sunset before we heard the engine burst into life. Later they continued working using the headlights of the jeep for some considerable time stripping the interior of the machine. Lee told us when he came for food that they were taking out all the extra seats and panelling in order to lighten the plane for take-off. They planned to take-off at first light the next morning.

March 23rd

Valerie and I had just finished breakfast when Lee arrived in the jeep. I thought he was returning it but he said Brad wanted to see us before they left. When we reached the aircraft the engine was already running and Brad was standing in the doorway. I was the last to step down from the jeep and Brad said something that I couldn't hear because of the plane's engine. However, I saw a look of horror on Lee's face as Brad pulled his arm from behind his back and pointed an automatic at him. That time I heard him. He said, 'You're too heavy Lee.'

His first shot hit Lee in the forehead and he was thrown back towards Valerie. I heard her scream then several shots were directed at us. There was no time to react. I felt a tremendous blow to my left shoulder and a sickening blow to my head.

I don't know how long I was unconscious but when I came to I couldn't see. There was blood running down my face and in my eyes, my left shoulder was numb and my left arm wouldn't work. I scraped some of the blood from my eyes and from my prone position I could then see the aircraft at the far end of the runway. I'm ashamed to admit it but at that instant I never gave Valerie or Lee any of my attention, my whole being was intent on stopping that bastard Brad.

For the next few minutes I believe I went mad. Behind me I could hear the engine note rising almost to a scream as Brad brought it up to full power with the brakes on. I knew he'd made a mistake and I could see what I wanted ahead of me but it felt as if I was crawling through treacle. The plane began to accelerate along the runway, the blood kept running into my eyes but I was determined to stop the swine. He was almost level with me when I fell onto the lever and the arrestor wires rose from the ground. The wheels hit the wires, the nose dropped, and the propeller hit the ground shattering into a thousand pieces. I was still screaming like a maniac as the plane dived into the lagoon at full power. I waited for him to surface but he never did.

Duncan found me four hours later. I was unconscious, sitting with my back propped against the jeep cradling Valerie's body in my arms. He thought I was dead as well. I nearly did die but Wong Kwee our elderly Chinese cook kept me alive until I was landed in Fiji. Duncan made all the arrangements for my medical treatment. I'm told I was landed at night and taken to a private clinic without the authorities being aware of my presence. He told me later that he'd done this because in my more lucid moments on the sea passage I'd babbled on about killing the pilot and wrecking the aircraft. He explained my bullet wounds as an accident while cleaning a gun but the doctor who treated me was well paid to keep silent.

July 19 1948

I'm well on the way to recovery now but I still feel weak at times. I have a steel plate holding my collarbone together and there's a white streak in my hair where the bullet creased my scalp. It's more or less a case of recovering my strength now, I'm still about a stone underweight but I'm told that is a vast improvement on what it was. I'd lost a tremendous amount of blood and had a raging fever when I was landed here so I suppose I'm lucky to be alive.

Mr Patel found me this room, it's in a guesthouse run by a friend of his. It is only small but it's clean and cheap. I've got a view out over the harbour here in Suva so I can watch the shipping movements. Duncan has brought Fat Tuesday in twice while I've been here and I've had visits from him and some of the other lads. I wanted to go aboard and thank Wonky for keeping me alive but he's left the ship now. They've got a new cook who apparently can't compete with the meals they enjoyed under Wonky's care but still serves up edible fare.

Duncan wants me to rejoin Fat Tuesday but I'm reluctant to do so. There are too many reminders of Valerie aboard her and I don't want to break down in front of my friends. I still wake up crying at night. I miss her terribly. Duncan buried her on the atoll. I must go back there. Last night I remembered what we were doing when that damned plane arrived — we, Valerie and I, had just had a naming ceremony for the islands. We were both tired of calling the place the Atoll so we re-named it. Those two islands and their attendant reefs are now called the Kingston Isles. I made a name board and nailed it to one of the posts by the jetty. Valerie christened it with a bottle of beer. That's when he heard that bloody plane.

I know I'm rambling on a bit but I wanted to record what I've remembered of those events in March. My memory keeps playing tricks on me; I keep remembering things out of sequence. The main thing is to record events as I remember them. This is the first time I've written anything since Valerie died and it has taken me all day to write these few pages.

July 20th 1948

Amongst the questions that are haunting me is why did that madman have to kill her? Why did he kill Lee? Why did he try to kill me? What was he trying to hide? There must have been something in that plane that he didn't want us to see. What was it? The answer must still lie with his remains in the bottom of the lagoon. I don't feel any guilt for killing him. I wonder if I should.

I've been spending a lot of time thinking about my future and I'm not sure what to do. Valerie wanted me to go back to England to visit my son. She had some idea that I should help with his upkeep more than I have been. It's difficult because he probably doesn't know I exist. I'll have to think about it when I'm fully fit. My health is improving but it is slow going. I started this diary again because although my body is slow my mind is racing. It might be something to do with being physically idle. It's years since I've been alone and out of work. There's nothing much to keep my mind occupied.

July 29th 1948

The harbourmaster left a message for me today. He's expecting Fat Tuesday to arrive tomorrow morning. I hope Duncan isn't in too much of a hurry because I want him to take me back to the Kingston Isles. I've had a small headstone made up and I'd like to put it on Valerie's grave. If he can't do it this trip then I'm prepared to wait until he can. I must go back and there's no other way of getting there.

I've taken up fishing to help me pass the time. I sit on the harbour wall and dangle a length of line into the water. I catch plenty of fish but I don't keep them. I just take them off the hook and toss them back. The locals think it's hilarious. I'm sure I caught the same fish three times this morning.

My shoulder is still very stiff despite my regular exercises. I'm hoping that if I keep going I can regain full movement eventually. At the moment I can only raise my arm to shoulder height.

July 30th 1948

Fat Tuesday arrived today and I didn't recognise her at first. Duncan has had her repainted — the hull is green and the upper-works are white. Just like those two landing craft we acquired. I don't know how he's done it but those two craft are now officially registered and have safety certificates and radio. Apparently all three vessels are in regular contact on high frequency radio. Duncan bought the radios at a military disposal sale and Harry fitted them onboard. The salvage part of the company has virtually gone and in its place is a legitimate trading company again.

I'm going back to the Kingston Isles, Duncan agreed to take me today. He'll take me there, wait for one day then bring me back here. He says that he has some slack in the system at the moment but as his trading contracts tighten up he won't have time to spare in future. The chandler is delivering the headstone to the ship today and I'll be going aboard this evening. I'm nervous, I don't know why but I am.

25

Jennifer told me later that she knew almost immediately that I had found something of real significance in Albert's notes. So much so that she put down the notebook she was reading and came to sit beside me to read over my shoulder. I felt her stiffen as she came to the part about the shootings then felt her tears dropping onto my shoulder as she tried to read on. I turned and held her to me as she wept for a woman she'd never known.

A few minutes later Jennifer went along to her cabin and I went up on deck. Joe was at the wheel and Kesa sat beside him. Kesa gave me a strange look then asked if Jennifer was okay.

'She'll be alright in a while. We've just found something rather upsetting in her grandfather's notes,' I replied.

'I warned you not to go disturbing old bones,' said Joe.

'Yes you did,' I agreed. 'Tell me Joe, did

you ever come across a vessel called *Fat Tuesday*?'

He nodded. 'Mr Fitzpatrick's schooner, she was driven ashore during a cyclone some years ago.'

'Where?' I exclaimed.

'Waya Island in the Yasawas, most of the crew was saved but the schooner was a total loss.'

'When was this?'

'About twenty years ago. The old man was the only casualty.'

'The old man?'

'Mr Fitzpatrick, it was his ship.'

'Which one, Duncan or Derek?'

'The old man, Duncan Fitzpatrick, Derek is still alive and visits Fiji regularly. His company has an office in Suva.'

'Why didn't I think to ask you earlier?' I said. 'We've been reading about the Fitzpatricks for days. They are part of the mystery we are trying to solve.'

'You two are talking as if Mr Derek Fitzpatrick is a young man,' Kesa exclaimed. 'He's at least eighty years old. I saw his picture in the paper only last week.'

'Yes, he must be,' I agreed. 'I've got a picture in my mind of a young man from reading about him but the notes I'm reading are fifty or sixty years old.'

'Old bones,' muttered Joe. 'I told you about old bones.'

Albert's notebook was still open on the table when I went below. There was no sign of Jennifer so I continued to read on through the notes. Judging by what he'd written Albert must have found the overnight stay on the islands an ordeal. He erected the headstone and sat beside the grave all that night. His notes spoke of a vigil and of prayers and apologies. I'm almost certain that he must have been on the verge of a nervous breakdown because he spoke of being jinxed. He actually wrote at one point of believing that any woman who was closely associated with him was sure to die young. This theme continued after his return to Fiji. His notes then were brief with long gaps between the entries but that theme of being jinxed persisted.

It wasn't until late in December 1948 that he seemed to pull himself together and regain a purpose in life. He wrote of hearing a carol service as he stood outside a church and of going in to listen. During that service he sat quietly at the back and, while he was there, he claimed Valerie spoke to him. She reminded him that he had a son, a boy who needed his attention. That boy became his purpose in life, his driving force for the next few years.

He was fully aware of the difficulties of moving money into and out of the United Kingdom as a result of the war, so early in the New Year he began to investigate the possibility of buying diamonds. His bank account was in good order with a healthy balance. The money he'd accumulated in the three years since the war had hardly been touched, largely because of living aboard the schooner and on the atoll. Valerie's earnings had been added when the pair married and they'd turned the account into a joint one. He was a comparatively rich man when viewed against men of a similar age and status back in England.

At the end of February 1949 he made

two entries of significance in his diary. The first was to confirm the purchase of the diamonds. However, he made no mention of their source. He merely stated that he'd bought them and intended to re-sell them in England. The money realised by their sale was to be for the benefit of his son. The second significant event was when he signed on as a fourth engineer on a British tramp steamer called *Atlantic Nomad*. He joined her because he was assured she was bound for England and nine months later she arrived in Liverpool.

In the years since the war Albert had sent the occasional food parcel from Australia to his brother's home. It wasn't until he joined *Atlantic Nomad* however that he became aware of the extent of rationing that still existed in Britain. His fellow seafarers regaled him with horror stories of food, fuel and clothing rationing that made him realise just how negligent he'd been to his son. After that he took every opportunity to send home parcels of food or clothing whenever the ship arrived in a new port.

During the nine months he spent aboard that ship he resumed the role of a quiet, competent seafarer. I think that period helped him recover from the shock of losing Valerie. I am almost certain that if he'd remained in Fiji at that time he'd have had a mental breakdown. The ship herself was true to her nomadic name, though she saw very little of Atlantic waters until the final few weeks of the voyage. Parcels arrived in the Beddows' household in Driffield from Sydney, Perth, Auckland, Madras, Singapore, Durban and Capetown. In those last two ports Albert purchased additional tinned food to take home on arrival in England. It was as if he was trying to make up for his perceived negligence of earlier years.

Some of the tinned food he had seems to have been used to divert the attention of the customs officer who searched his cabin in Liverpool. The officer left with two tins of fruit having found no contraband. Throughout the search Albert sat quietly smoking and reading, with the diamonds secreted in a matchbox in his pocket. He lost a further tin of fruit at the dockyard gate as the policeman on duty checked his luggage but once again the diamonds went undetected.

His arrival at Brian's house was completely unannounced. Although he had sent food parcels from various ports he had never written a letter to his brother in all the time he had been abroad. Despite his lack of communication he was well received by all three members of his brother's household. He described his son David as a polite young schoolboy who had addressed him as Uncle Albert. Brenda, Brian's wife, was effusive in her thanks for the food parcels and the tinned food he'd brought from South Africa but spent an anxious few hours until Albert assured her that he had no intention of removing David from her care. He stayed with them two days before moving to the seamen's mission in Hull.

For the next three days he walked around the city trying to find a jeweller who looked affluent enough to purchase the diamonds. However, there was so much bomb damage to the centre that he struggled to find a jeweller at all. In the end he decided to look in another town. He picked York simply because when he walked into Paragon railway station the next morning there was a train leaving for there ten minutes later. In York he allowed his instinct to take over and direct him to what he felt was the right shop. Mr Phillip's shop was the second one he came to. He didn't waste any time on preliminaries, he simply walked into the shop and asked to see the owner. I remembered old Mr Phillip's description of their meeting.

'I am the proprietor,' John Phillips.

'Do you buy diamonds, Mr Phillips?'

'I do if they are legal.'

'The diamonds I have for sale were legally purchased by me.'

'May I see them?'

Albert took the matchbox from his pocket, slid it open and allowed the jeweller to select one stone. It happened to be one of the two yellow diamonds. There was a sharp intake of breath as Phillips examined the stone through an eyeglass. Albert allowed the examination to continue stone by stone until each had been carefully scrutinized, weighed and replaced. Eventually Phillips looked up and removed the eyeglass.

'How much?' he asked.

'One thousand pounds.'

'They are worth more than that.'

'I know, but I'm leaving the country in a couple of days and I can't take them with me.'

Phillips nodded, thought for a few moments then made his decision. 'I'll have to go to the bank,' he said. 'Can you come back in an hour?'

Albert agreed and left the shop with his diamonds safely back in his pocket. He stopped in a convenient doorway and waited until Phillips locked his shop door and walked off along the street. Albert followed unobtrusively, watched as he entered the bank and waited until he emerged thirty minutes later. Back at the shop the diamonds were checked once again before being exchanged for a wad of crisp white five-pound notes.

The following day Albert travelled to his brother's home again and handed over a bank-book to his astonished sibling. Apart from retaining fifty pounds for his own immediate expenses he had banked the rest of the diamond money in an account to be used for David's education. He left Hull three days later aboard a ship bound for Australia. He signed-on as a fourth engineer yet again.

26

I couldn't find a diary or notebook covering the 1950/51 period but a new diary began in January 1952. By that time he was in Auckland, New Zealand and was busy refitting a yacht that he had bought. The yacht was *Island Beauty* and from the description of the work he'd done it sounded as if a major refit had been required. He talked of a complete engine change and new sail rigs to enable him to sail the vessel single-handed. He was also experimenting with shallow water diving using basic scuba equipment acquired from the U.S. Navy.

By the end of February he was doing sea trials with his newly refurbished yacht. There were some minor problems to sort out as a result of the trials but by the middle of March he was storing the vessel ready for a prolonged voyage. He eventually sailed from Auckland on the 20th March 1952 bound for Suva in Fiji.

Although no mention was made of it in his notes at that time it seemed obvious to me that his ultimate destination was the Kingston Isles.

In this day and age with yachtsmen circumnavigating the globe on a regular basis it is hard to imagine what a tremendous undertaking Albert's first single-handed voyage was. True, he'd been a seaman all his working life but he had worked as an engineer. The only navigating experience he'd had was when he'd interchanged his working environment with the fellow members of *Fat Tuesday's* crew. However, he made a successful passage to Suva where he renewed his contacts with the Patel family and with the crew of *Fat Tuesday*.

I think he deliberately waited in Suva for *Fat Tuesday* to arrive because he spent some considerable time with Duncan discussing the Kingston Islands. It was patently obvious from his notes that he had every intention of heading straight for the islands because he had discussed the best course to take, how to line up for the passage through the reef and the safest anchorage positions. Once again he took onboard a considerable quantity of tinned, dried and fresh provisions. He appeared to be preparing for a long stay.

It was mid-August when he eventually anchored in the lagoon. Although he had timed his approach in order to anchor in daylight he made no attempt to land on that first day. Instead he surveyed the islands through binoculars noting changes that had occurred over the years since his last visit. He seemed surprised by the amount of new growth especially on what had been the runway. New trees and shrubs made it impossible for any aircraft to land there again.

He went ashore on the second day and spent his first hours clearing the area around Valerie's grave. Once again he noted with some surprise the density of the new growth. Later he walked the length of both islands paying particular attention to the abandoned garden area. He also confirmed that the bulldozer still sat by what had once been the runway. The machine was almost hidden in undergrowth and covered in rust but Albert considered it worth salvaging.

It took him almost a week to coax life back into the bulldozer. He then spent several days driving the machine back and forth clearing a roadway from the boat landing stage back across the bridge and down to the end of the old runway. His next target for his clearance operation was the overgrown garden area. Not only did he partially clear it but he also replanted it with seeds that he'd brought from Fiji. He'd already checked that the rainwater storage tanks left by the Americans were still fully operational so there was no danger of him dying of thirst or hunger no matter how long he chose to stay. However, he elected to live aboard the yacht rather than to move into the accommodation that he and Valerie had shared ashore.

I think he had every intention of trying to pull the wrecked aircraft back onto the runway using the bulldozer. He certainly prepared for such an attempt by clearing the land at that end of the runway and by taking tow ropes from the yacht. However, when he made his first dive on the wreck three weeks after his arrival he quickly changed his mind. The aircraft was apparently in several pieces. One wing lay on the reef only a few feet below the surface but the remainder of the machine lay in deeper water.

That first dive was simply an initial inspection and he wasn't wearing scuba gear merely a snorkel and mask. I don't know what he was expecting to find but his diary records his disappointment. He'd left Fiji with six charged air bottles for his scuba gear but he had no means of recharging them. The fact that the aircraft was deeper than he was expecting and in pieces meant that he would have to ration his available air very carefully. He had no idea what he was looking for but he was certain that something of importance lay in the wreck. The wreck however lay scattered in pieces across the bottom of the lagoon making the search more difficult.

On his second dive he wore scuba gear but with only one air bottle. He remained underwater for almost half an hour examining the different parts of the wreck. His diary records the fact that the remains of the pilot were still *in situ* in the cockpit. The cockpit itself remained attached to the engine compartment and the stub of the starboard wing, the section lay about forty feet from the rest of the wreck. The fuselage was in two pieces adjacent to what was left of the tailfin and the starboard wing. Sand had drifted over and into the wreckage whilst weed and barnacles had begun to transform it into a living entity. He recorded the depth of water over the wreck site as approximately thirty feet.

It wasn't until his fifth dive almost two weeks later that he began to find what he'd been looking for. Close to what remained of the fuselage he spotted the handle of a suitcase protruding from the sandy seabed. He painstakingly eased the sand away from the handle only to discover that it was attached to a small fraction of what had been a suitcase. However, as he brushed away the sand his attention was diverted by a sudden gleam of gold. He surfaced a few minutes later clutching a small gold ingot that fitted neatly into the palm of his hand. Although he couldn't be certain it was gold the weight of the ingot encouraged him to believe that it was.

Later, back on board the yacht, he assessed his situation. He had only enough air for one more dive but he now felt that the aircraft had been carrying something of considerable value. That something lay scattered across the floor of the lagoon beneath a covering of sand. He would need time to search the seabed thoroughly and his one charged air-bottle was clearly insufficient for that purpose. His decision was to make one final dive the following day before returning to Fiji.

Before that final dive he manufactured a short handled rake by hammering eight six-inch nails through a piece of wood and attaching a handle to it. It was only a crude affair but it proved sufficient to rake through the sand and unearth more finds. In the time his limited air supply allowed him he raked over a few square feet of the sandy bottom close to where he'd found the ingot the day before. His first find was a gold half sovereign and his second a tin tobacco box sealed with solder. Once back onboard Albert used a small hacksaw to open the sealed box, inside he found a small leather pouch holding a collection of green stones which later proved to be emeralds. There were seven stones altogether, the main one being the size of his thumb-nail, the others were about half that size. All seven were cut and polished as if they had once formed part of a necklace or tiara.

Knowing that he could not continue with his underwater search without charged air bottles Albert had to return to Fiji if he wished to continue diving on the wreck. However, before he did so, he took the precaution of greasing and oiling every moving part on the bulldozer that he could. He then parked it in the shelter of one of the prefabricated buildings, one that had been used by the Americans as a machine shop. He actually had no further use for the bulldozer but his engineering instincts wouldn't allow him to abandon it again.

27

Jennifer and I had our first glimpse of the Kingston Isles through binoculars late in the afternoon. It was frustrating to be able to see them but be unable to land. However, Joe wasn't prepared to attempt to enter the lagoon so late in the day. I could understand his caution because no ship master would enter a strange anchorage with darkness approaching and no lights on the shore to guide him.

Earlier that day I had examined the yacht's diving equipment. There were six sets of scuba gear and an air compressor. Both Seru and Kesa were fully qualified divers. I had qualified during my time in the Navy but in recent years hadn't done much underwater work at all. Jennifer assured me that she was a good swimmer but had never dived. She had however used a snorkel and mask during holidays. I had every intention of investigating what was left of the aircraft wreckage so I explained to Joe and Seru what I planned to do. Seru was full of enthusiasm and immediately offered to dive with me. Joe on the other hand trotted out his usual statement about not disturbing old bones.

Joe waited for full daylight the following morning before attempting to enter the lagoon. By that time all the sails had been lowered and stowed. As we approached the entrance with the main engine running at slow speed Joe had the wheel whilst Seru watched the echo sounder carefully. It was obvious to me that they were well practised at making similar approaches in uncertain waters. Their quiet confidence was reassuring and merely served to emphasise that we had made the correct choice of vessel and crew. Once inside the lagoon Kesu moved to the echo sounder and Seru went forward to release the anchor.

The rattle of the anchor cable was accompanied by screams of protest from the islands' feathered population. However, a few minutes later, after the initial protest had subsided, the only sounds were those of the surf caressing the reef and occasional slap of the rigging against the mast. All five of us stood in silence gazing towards the shore. I cleared my throat and it was as if I'd given a signal to start talking.

'Well, we've arrived,' said Seru.

'There're signs of recent storm damage,' muttered Joe as he peered through narrowed eyes at the larger of the islands.

'It's beautiful,' Jennifer murmured, 'Grandfather's paradise.' She turned to me. 'I want to explore, how soon can we go ashore?'

Behind me Seru chuckled. 'I'll put a boat in the water while you're having breakfast,' he said.

Despite its age the jetty that Albert had first stepped on almost sixty years ago was still in remarkably good condition. The timber decking was green and slippery in places but the basic structure still felt firm underfoot. I tested its strength before assisting Jennifer from the boat. While I was securing the painter she walked to the end of the jetty. She was gazing up at a faded wooden sign when I rejoined her. There were tears in her eyes as she surveyed her Grandfather's handiwork. The words had been chiselled out of the board so that they were still clearly visible despite the fact that paint had long since faded and flaked. It simply said, 'The Kingston Islands'.

I knew from Albert's notes that a road of crushed coral had run alongside the water's edge and had connected with the bridge that led to the second island. However, nature had taken over and trees and shrubs had colonised the road in places. Many of the trees now lay horizontally across what remained of the road having been torn bodily from the ground by storm force winds. A number of the buildings had also collapsed. While I was still surveying the damage Jennifer moved alongside me and took my hand.

'Where is Valerie buried?' she asked.

'I think the grave is over there, just to the right of that building.'

I led the way and after scrambling over two of the fallen trees I found the headstone. The grave was somewhat overgrown but the granite stone was clearly visible. Jennifer knelt and began to pull at the grass and weeds with her bare hands. I put my hand on her shoulder and said, 'Leave it for now Jenny. If you want to tidy it up we can bring some tools tomorrow and make a good job of it.'

It was then that I realised she was crying and that her attempts at tidying the grave were intended to hide that fact from me. I left her kneeling there and walked over to study the adjacent building. This was the building that Albert and Valerie had lived in so long ago. In his notes Albert had said that they'd picked this particular one because it was much stronger than many of the others. He was obviously right because most of the others had collapsed and their remains had been taken over by rampant tropical greenery of one kind or another.

Jennifer rejoined me and held my hand once again. We walked along what remained of the road, scrambling over fallen trees until we reached the bridge connecting the two islands. The bridge reminded me of the Bailey bridges used by our armed forces. Its main structure was of steel girders bolted together whilst the roadway was of heavy timbers similar to railway sleepers. Once again the timber was green and slippery but the rest of the structure was in fine condition apart from a layer of rust. It looked as if it would last for many more years.

It was hard to imagine that the second island had ever been an airfield because it too was covered in tropical growth. Again many of the trees had been flattened by storm force winds but newer growth was already springing up in their place. I recognised coconut palms and papaya but although others looked familiar I couldn't name them.

Without consciously doing so I had led the way towards the end of the island where the aircraft had come to grief so long ago. It wasn't until I stumbled over a metal lever sticking upright from the ground that I realised where we were.

'It must be the lever that operated the arrestor wires,' I said as I bent to massage my bruised shin.

Jennifer looked around. 'Valerie died

near here,' she said quietly.

'I think that place must be underwater now, do you remember what Jimmy Footweller said about Lee's grave being washed away. Look where the high water mark is now, only a few feet away. This island must be about half the size it was when Valerie was killed.'

'Why is that?'

I shrugged my shoulders. 'Global warming,' I suggested.

Jennifer nodded. 'I think I've seen enough for today, let's go back,' she said.

I glanced at my watch and realised with a shock that we had been on the islands over four hours. Originally I'd intended to take a short walk to inspect the layout but we'd both been so intent on tying together what we'd read in Albert's notes and what we were seeing at first hand that time had slipped away unnoticed. By the time we reached the boat I was feeling hot, tired and hungry and I could see that Jennifer felt exactly the same.

Back on the yacht we shared a sandwich and beer lunch that Kesa had prepared when she'd seen us heading back. Afterwards I had a long shower and an even longer siesta. Jennifer must have done something similar because it was almost sunset before either of us put in an appearance again.

28

That evening we decided on our movements for the next day. Although I had
earlier volunteered to help Jennifer with
tidying the area around Valerie's grave
Seru thought it wiser that I got in some
dive practise. Kesa agreed to accompany
Jennifer whilst I renewed my acquain-
tance with scuba gear. I hadn't dived for
some years and Seru felt that I needed
some practise in the waters around the
yacht before attempting to dive on the
aircraft wreck. I agreed with him and
Jennifer seemed happy enough with the
change of plan.

The following morning Seru insisted
that we checked every piece of equipment
together and agreed on our underwater
hand signals before we entered the water.
Our first dive lasted twenty minutes
although at the time it seemed to me to
be over much quicker. I think Seru
wanted reassurance that I knew what I

was doing before he was prepared for deeper and longer dives as my buddy. I respected him for that.

Jennifer and Kesa returned from the shore before lunch and it was then that Seru pronounced himself ready to dive on the wreck with me. Kesa and Jennifer were to accompany us in the dive boat but remain on the surface although Kesa would be equipped for diving in the unlikely event of an emergency.

On our initial dive we had seen hundreds of brightly coloured fish but no sharks. However, as the lagoon was open to the sea there was every possibility that we could meet some during our next dive. We both carried knives and underwater flares but for this deeper dive Seru armed himself with a spear-gun. The spear-gun was what he called a last resort weapon, a weapon that under normal circumstances he wouldn't contemplate using. He advised punching any over curious shark on the nose to scare it off but as I had never encountered a shark before I was nervous about that advice and comforted by the sight of that ugly looking weapon.

It was hard for us to estimate where the remains of the aircraft lay because of the way that the sea had encroached on the islands. In Albert's notes the wreck lay just off the end of the runway but now we had no way of knowing just where that was. In any case from the evidence of storm damage on the shore there was every possibility that the wreck site may have been disturbed in that same storm. We would in effect be diving blind, just hoping to find something to corroborate Albert's story in the short time that we'd allocated ourselves.

Most of my diving experience had been amassed in cold northern waters where to encounter a shark was something of a rarity. There are some of course but the majority are basking sharks that pose no threat to divers since they feed on plankton. However, the shark that I encountered on that first big dive in the lagoon was long, lean and looked decidedly dangerous. I was following Seru down towards the bottom of the lagoon when the creature slid between us. I suppose I was more surprised than anything else because I hadn't seen it coming and it slid past my nose with only a couple of feet to spare. It circled us twice but sheered off and disappeared when Seru released a stream of air bubbles as it passed over him.

We found nothing on that first dive nor on our second the following day. However, on the third day we began to find aircraft remains. I did not expect to find any of the treasure trove that Albert had recovered. Instead I wanted to find some form of identification mark on what remained of the aircraft. Albert had made no attempt to identify the pilot or his companion but I felt that we should do so if at all possible. Seru and I were therefore searching for serial numbers on any part of the aircraft we found. The engine block was clearly identifiable but because of the coral and weed growth on and around it we never found what we were looking for.

The frame of the cockpit was still intact but the window glass had long since disappeared. There was no sign of human remains but some of the cockpit controls could still be identified. The control panel was still there but it was so coated in barnacles and weed growth that it was impossible to identify any instruments. However, I felt that if we could cut part of it away and get it back onboard then we may eventually find serial numbers. Despite our best efforts we never found the wings or the tailplane.

On our fourth and final dive on the wreck Seru and I armed ourselves with bolt cutters, a hacksaw and net attached to a line. We were able to cut away roughly half of the control panel with comparative ease although at that stage we couldn't tell just what was hidden in the lumps of concretion that coated the instruments. As we loaded the net with the battered remains of the panel I realised that I'd left the bolt cutters behind.

Whilst Seru watched as the net was hauled up by Kesa I returned for the tools. At first I couldn't find the cutters and I only did so by accident. They'd dropped clear of the cockpit and lay partially buried in the sandy bottom and I found them by standing on them. As I groped in the sand my fingers encountered something else, a small metal plate. I could feel the indentations as I ran my fingers over the surface and I suddenly realised we had found what we were searching for; that tiny plate held a series of numbers. I could hardly believe it, we'd searched in vain for serial numbers and just when we'd given up I'd found one by accident. Although it wasn't attached to the aircraft it could only have come from there.

On our way back to the yacht Seru and I discussed the possibility of another dive the following day. Our intention was to gently comb the sand around what remained of the aircraft to see if we could unearth any other small finds. However, Joe soon put an end to our speculation. The barometer had begun to indicate a change of weather and despite the reports that the anchorage was safe in bad weather Joe was uneasy about remaining there in a storm. He did agree somewhat reluctantly to wait until the following morning but when that dawned grey and wet with squally winds he refused to wait any longer.

We sailed through the gap in the reef straight after breakfast. Jennifer was happy that she had seen all that she wanted to see of the islands so we set off on the return journey to Fiji immediately. With a following wind of near gale force and a rising sea we had something of a rollercoaster ride throughout that day. During the night however the wind began to ease and by the following morning was down to force three. The sea was still rather lumpy but even that settled down as the day advanced. Joe was convinced that the storm front had passed to the north of us, probably across the islands we had just left.

29

It was on the third day of our return passage that we began work on the battered remains of the control panel. Both Jennifer and I spent the morning gently chipping away at the concretion covering the instruments. It was slow work but by that evening we had uncovered what appeared to be an oil gauge. Unfortunately we couldn't see any identifying numbers. By that time my finger ends were feeling extremely tender. I had worn gloves when we started work but they were too cumbersome so I'd dispensed with them.

The following morning Kesa produced a selection of thin rubber gloves taken from the yacht's medical kit. They proved fine enough for us to work in reasonable comfort without hampering our movements. That day we uncovered an altimeter and it carried a clearly identifiable serial number. We found nothing else recognisable on what remained of the section of salvaged instrument panel. However, the two instruments that we had recovered were both American in origin.

It seemed like a long shot but Jennifer and I talked it over and decided to consult our one American contact to see if we had enough to identify the aircraft's origin. Allowing for the time difference between the South Pacific and England I waited until ten o'clock that night before ringing Jimmy Footweller in London. If he was surprised to hear from us he didn't sound it and the satellite telephone connection was clear and noise free. It took me a few minutes to explain just what we had found and he seemed particularly interested in the small metal plate I'd found in the sand. He took the details of everything we'd discovered and promised to be in touch as soon as he had any news. I wasn't expecting him to find anything after such a long time but he appeared to be positive and almost enthusiastic about what we'd found.

Only half an hour after we'd finished

that call he rang back. His interest in the metal plate we'd found now centred on its size, he wanted its exact dimensions. He didn't explain why despite our curiosity.

It took us one day less to get back to Fiji than it had taken on the way out. The prevailing trade winds pushed the yacht along at a good speed. During that return journey I took every opportunity that I could to take the wheel and I even managed to persuade Jennifer to do the same. I'm sure that as her confidence grew she also began to enjoy being at the controls of such a fine vessel. I think she may even have contemplated sailing her own yacht because she began asking questions about the cost of moorings and fuel. However, she never openly stated what was in her mind at that time despite my gentle probing.

One of the things I found remarkable about the whole voyage out and back was the way I lost complete track of the days. I thought about it on the night before we arrived back in Fiji and suddenly realised that I hadn't a clue what day it was or what date. When I was in the Navy I'd always known both day and date because of having to maintain the ship's logbook but there in the South Pacific that duty belonged to someone else. I remember asking Jennifer what day it was and her answer didn't surprise me.

'It doesn't seem to matter,' she said. 'I'm thoroughly enjoying the whole experience of being away from television, newspapers and the usual rat race.'

After dinner that evening we sat together out on deck. We, Jennifer and I, were up forward whilst Joe had the wheel. The yacht was still sliding smoothly along under sail and apart from the hiss of the water along the hull there was no noise. It was one of those magical warm tropical nights with a full moon and millions of stars above us. Neither of us was inclined to talk, we just sat close together enjoying both the evening and each other's company. I think it was the realisation that the cruise was shortly to end that affected us both. We must have been there nearly an hour when I suddenly felt a drop of water on my hand. At first I thought it was spray but then I saw a tear trickle down Jennifer's face. I put my arm around her and drew her to me. We slept in each other's arms that night.

The last person I was expecting to greet us on our arrival back in Fiji was Jimmy Footweller but there he was, as large as life, standing on the shore alongside the immigration officer. Once the arrival formalities had finished Jimmy was the first man aboard. Once the introductions were over he got straight down to business.

'May I see your finds?' he said.

We were sitting at the saloon table at the time and when I placed the battered instruments and the small metal plate in front of him he smiled and nodded.

'I thought so,' he said picking up the small plate. 'It's not from a machine. This is part of a serviceman's identity tag.'

'That's why you're here — you know who it belonged to,' exclaimed Jennifer.

'Yes, a deserter from the United States Navy, a pilot who went missing in Japan just after the second-world-war.'

'What was his name?' I asked.

'Bradley Ostermeyer, an American of Dutch descent, he was a civilian pilot before the war and volunteered for the Navy at the time of Pearl Harbour.'

At the time of his disappearance Bradley Ostermeyer was part of a team of U.S. officers who were interrogating Japanese military personnel. Lee was thought to be one of those Japanese officers and he had disappeared at the same time as Ostermeyer. Lee had fought in China and the Philippines and was suspected of knowing the whereabouts of a large hoard of looted material.

'So what my grandfather recovered from the wreck was looted during the war,' said Jennifer.

'Probably,' replied Jimmy, 'but after all this time we have no means of checking, especially when you consider that the jewellery in particular appears to have been broken down. The one identifiable piece was the golden chess piece but no one seems to know who owned it when the war started. It was originally lost in Russia.'

'Did Ostermeyer know about the atoll

or was it pure chance that he landed there?' I asked.

'He certainly knew about it, he'd landed a damaged aircraft there during the war.'

'Where did they get the aircraft?'

Jimmy shrugged. 'Who knows,' he replied, 'maybe from the same place as the hidden loot.'

'What happens now?' Jennifer asked.

'We pack our bags, say our goodbyes and head for home I suppose,' I said.

Jimmy nodded. 'All I need is this to close a file on a Navy deserter,' he said holding up the identification tag.

30

Jennifer and I flew back to London three days later but we didn't travel north together. Jimmy Footweller had requested my presence at the embassy in order to put together a formal report about the finding of the identity tag. Since I was already in London it seemed pointless travelling north and returning a few days later to see Jimmy so I escorted Jennifer to her connecting flight to Leeds/Bradford airport before checking into a hotel.

There was more to Jimmy's request than I had anticipated. He certainly wanted a detailed report of the location of the aircraft wreckage and the identity tag but he also had a proposition for me. He asked me to return to the atoll on a U.S. Naval vessel to act as a liaison officer for a diving team to make a more thorough investigation of the wreck site. The request took me by surprise but I agreed to do it. I remained in London three days and because of that I missed Jennifer. As I left London to head up to Yorkshire she was leaving home to visit her agent in London.

Despite my best efforts to arrange a meeting Jennifer and I didn't get together again for almost three months. When I got back from the second trip to the atoll Jennifer was in Switzerland arranging the sale of the gemstones that remained in the bank vaults. We talked on the telephone occasionally but I became increasingly aware of a distancing in our relationship. When we finally did have dinner together it was because Jennifer wanted me to arrange for her grandfather's yacht to be moved and sold.

The American diving team did a thoroughly professional search of the crash site turning up a number of gold coins in the process. They managed to identify the aircraft as one built in America in 1940 and flown out to Manila that same year. It was later captured by the invading Japanese forces. There was no known record of it after that time until it turned up at the atoll.

As a result of the photographs and sketches that Jennifer produced on and after our Pacific jaunt her career as a book illustrator and artist took off. She began to receive commissions of a much more lucrative nature and as her career blossomed our contact diminished. We have remained friends but apart from the occasional meal together out relationship has never returned to the one we enjoyed for that short period in the South Pacific. Was it just a shipboard romance or something I said or did wrong? I don't suppose I'll ever know now — her engagement to a fellow artist was announced in the local press yesterday.

The odd thing is that while I was reading the engagement notice my door-bell rang. I signed for and collected a parcel delivered by a local courier service. It contained a golden chess piece, the very piece that had started our adventure. The accompanying note simply said 'Thank You' — it was signed 'Jenny'.

We do hope that you have enjoyed reading this large print book.

Did you know that all of our titles are available for purchase?

We publish a wide range of high quality large print books including:
Romances, Mysteries, Classics
General Fiction
Non Fiction and Westerns

Special interest titles available in large print are:
The Little Oxford Dictionary
Music Book, Song Book
Hymn Book, Service Book

Also available from us courtesy of Oxford University Press:
Young Readers' Dictionary
(large print edition)
Young Readers' Thesaurus
(large print edition)

For further information or a free brochure, please contact us at:
Ulverscroft Large Print Books Ltd.,
The Green, Bradgate Road, Anstey,
Leicester, LE7 7FU, England.
Tel: (00 44) **0116 236 4325**
Fax: (00 44) **0116 234 0205**